KLINCK MEMORIAL LIBRARY
Concordia College
River Forest, IL 60305

Earth's Enigmas

"TWO GRAY LEOPARDS AND A SMALL APE."
(See page 120)

Earth's Enigmas

By
SIR CHARLES GEORGE DOUGLAS ROBERTS

ILLUSTRATED BY
Charles Livingston Bull

KLINCK MEMORIAL LIBRARY
Concordia College
River Forest, IL 60305

Short Story Index Reprint Series

BOOKS FOR LIBRARIES PRESS
FREEPORT, NEW YORK

First Published 1895
Reprinted 1969

STANDARD BOOK NUMBER:
8369-3122-X

LIBRARY OF CONGRESS CATALOG CARD NUMBER:
72-94742

BY
HALLMARK LITHOGRAPHERS, INC.

Prefatory Note.

Most of the stories in this collection attempt to present one or another of those problems of life or nature to which, as it appears to many of us, there is no adequate solution within sight. Others are the almost literal transcript of dreams which seemed to me to have a coherency, completeness, and symbolic significance sufficiently marked to justify me in setting them down. The rest are scenes from that simple life of Canadian backwoods and tide-country with which my earlier years made me familiar.

This edition is enlarged by the

inclusion of three new stories, entitled "The House at Stony Lonesome," "The Hill of Chastisement," and "On the Tantramar Dyke;" and what is more important, it is enriched by the drawings of Mr. Charles Livingston Bull, for whose sympathetic interpretations I take this opportunity of expressing my gratitude.

C. G. D. R.

New York, April, 1903.

Contents

	PAGE
Do Seek their Meat from God	11
Within Sound of the Saws	28
"The Young Ravens that Call upon Him"	56
Strayed	66
The Butt of the Camp	76
At the Rough-and-Tumble Landing	97
In the Accident Ward	119
The Perdu	124
The Romance of an Ox-Team	158
On the Tantramar Dyke	181
The Hill of Chastisement	197
Captain Joe and Jamie	204
The Barn on the Marsh	220
The Stone Dog	232
Stony-Lonesome	250

List of Illustrations

	PAGE
"Two gray leopards and a small ape" (*See page 120*)	*Frontispiece*
"Out of a shadowy hollow behind a long, white rock ... came softly a great panther"	12
"The lamb hung limp from his talons"	64
"He saw, dimly, the tawny brute"	74
"A moveless statue of a bird"	138
"Slouching inertly along the narrow backwoods road"	158
"As I set forth the gloom deepened"	200
"How the wind roared in from the sea!"	204
"There, hung the dead body of our neighbor"	222
"From whose eye a dull white glow seemed just vanishing"	240

Earth's Enigmas.

Do Seek their Meat from God.

ONE side of the ravine was in darkness. The darkness was soft and rich, suggesting thick foliage. Along the crest of the slope tree-tops came into view — great pines and hemlocks of the ancient unviolated forest — revealed against the orange disk of a full moon just rising. The low rays slanting through the moveless tops lit strangely the upper portion of the opposite steep, — the western wall of the ravine, barren, unlike its fellow, bossed with great rocky pro-

Do seek their meat from God jections, and harsh with stunted junipers. Out of the sluggish dark that lay along the ravine as in a trough, rose the brawl of a swollen, obstructed stream.

Out of a shadowy hollow behind a long white rock, on the lower edge of that part of the steep which lay in the moonlight, came softly a great panther. In common daylight his coat would have shown a warm fulvous hue, but in the elvish decolorizing rays of that half hidden moon he seemed to wear a sort of spectral gray. He lifted his smooth round head to gaze on the increasing flame, which presently he greeted with a shrill cry. That terrible cry, at once plaintive and menacing, with an undertone like the fierce protestations of a saw beneath the file, was a summons to his mate, telling her that the hour had come when they should seek their prey. From the lair behind the rock, where the cubs

"OUT OF A SHADOWY HOLLOW BEHIND A LONG, WHITE ROCK . . . CAME SOFTLY A GREAT PANTHER."

were being suckled by their dam, *Do seek*
came no immediate answer. Only a *their meat*
pair of crows, that had their nest in *from God*
a giant fir-tree across the gulf, woke
up and croaked harshly their indignation. These three summers past
they had built in the same spot, and
had been nightly awakened to vent
the same rasping complaints.

The panther walked restlessly up
and down, half a score of paces each
way, along the edge of the shadow,
keeping his wide-open green eyes
upon the rising light. His short,
muscular tail twitched impatiently,
but he made no sound. Soon the
breadth of confused brightness had
spread itself further down the steep,
disclosing the foot of the white rock,
and the bones and antlers of a deer
which had been dragged thither and
devoured.

By this time the cubs had made
their meal, and their dam was ready
for such enterprise as must be ac-

Do seek their meat from God complished ere her own hunger, now grown savage, could hope to be assuaged. She glided supplely forth into the glimmer, raised her head, and screamed at the moon in a voice as terrible as her mate's. Again the crows stirred, croaking harshly; and the two beasts, noiselessly mounting the steep, stole into the shadows of the forest that clothed the high plateau.

The panthers were fierce with hunger. These two days past their hunting had been wellnigh fruitless. What scant prey they had slain had for the most part been devoured by the female; for had she not those small blind cubs at home to nourish, who soon must suffer at any lack of hers? The settlements of late had been making great inroads on the world of ancient forest, driving before them the deer and smaller game. Hence the sharp hunger of the panther parents, and hence it came that on this night they hunted *Do seek* together. They purposed to steal *their meat* upon the settlements in their sleep, *from God* and take tribute of the enemies' flocks.

Through the dark of the thick woods, here and there pierced by the moonlight, they moved swiftly and silently. Now and again a dry twig would snap beneath the discreet and padded footfalls. Now and again, as they rustled some low tree, a pewee or a nuthatch would give a startled chirp. For an hour the noiseless journeying continued, and ever and anon the two gray, sinuous shapes would come for a moment into the view of the now well-risen moon. Suddenly there fell upon their ears, far off and faint, but clearly defined against the vast stillness of the Northern forest, a sound which made those stealthy hunters pause and lift their heads. It was the voice of a child crying, — crying

<small>*Do seek their meat from God*</small> long and loud, hopelessly, as if there were no one by to comfort it. The panthers turned aside from their former course and glided toward the sound. They were not yet come to the outskirts of the settlement, but they knew of a solitary cabin lying in the thick of the woods a mile and more from the nearest neighbor. Thither they bent their way, fired with fierce hope. Soon would they break their bitter fast.

Up to noon of the previous day the lonely cabin had been occupied. Then its owner, a shiftless fellow, who spent his days for the most part at the corner tavern three miles distant, had suddenly grown disgusted with a land wherein one must work to live, and had betaken himself with his seven-year-old boy to seek some more indolent clime. During the long lonely days when his father was away at the tavern the little boy had been wont to visit the house of the next neighbor, to play *Do seek* with a child of some five summers, *their meat* who had no other playmate. The *from God* next neighbor was a prosperous pioneer, being master of a substantial frame house in the midst of a large and well-tilled clearing. At times, though rarely, because it was forbidden, the younger child would make his way by a rough wood road to visit his poor little disreputable playmate. At length it had appeared that the five-year-old was learning unsavory language from the elder boy, who rarely had an opportunity of hearing speech more desirable. To the bitter grief of both children, the companionship had at length been stopped by unalterable decree of the master of the frame house.

Hence it had come to pass that the little boy was unaware of his comrade's departure. Yielding at last to an eager longing for that comrade, he had stolen away late in the

Do seek their meat from God afternoon, traversed with endless misgivings the lonely stretch of wood road, and reached the cabin only to find it empty. The door, on its leathern hinges, swung idly open. The one room had been stripped of its few poor furnishings. After looking in the rickety shed, whence darted two wild and hawklike chickens, the child had seated himself on the hacked threshold, and sobbed passionately with a grief that he did not fully comprehend. Then seeing the shadows lengthen across the tiny clearing, he had grown afraid to start for home. As the dusk gathered, he had crept trembling into the cabin, whose door would not stay shut. When it grew quite dark, he crouched in the inmost corner of the room, desperate with fear and loneliness, and lifted up his voice piteously. From time to time his lamentations would be choked by sobs, or he would grow breathless, and in the terrifying silence would listen hard to hear if *Do seek their meat from God* any one or anything were coming. Then again would the shrill childish wailings arise, startling the unexpectant night, and piercing the forest depths, even to the ears of those great beasts which had set forth to seek their meat from God.

The lonely cabin stood some distance, perhaps a quarter of a mile, back from the highway connecting the settlements. Along this main road a man was plodding wearily. All day he had been walking, and now as he neared home his steps began to quicken with anticipation of rest. Over his shoulder projected a double-barrelled fowling-piece, from which was slung a bundle of such necessities as he had purchased in town that morning. It was the prosperous settler, the master of the frame house. His mare being with foal, he had chosen to make the tedious journey on foot.

Do seek their meat from God The settler passed the mouth of the wood road leading to the cabin. He had gone perhaps a furlong beyond, when his ears were startled by the sound of a child crying in the woods. He stopped, lowered his burden to the road, and stood straining ears and eyes in the direction of the sound. It was just at this time that the two panthers also stopped, and lifted their heads to listen. Their ears were keener than those of the man, and the sound had reached them at a greater distance.

Presently the settler realized whence the cries were coming. He called to mind the cabin; but he did not know the cabin's owner had departed. He cherished a hearty contempt for the drunken squatter; and on the drunken squatter's child he looked with small favor, especially as a playmate for his own boy. Nevertheless he hesitated before resuming his journey.

"Poor little devil!" he muttered, half in wrath. "I reckon his precious father's drunk down at 'the Corners,' and him crying for loneliness!" Then he reshouldered his burden and strode on doggedly.

Do seek their meat from God

But louder, shriller, more hopeless and more appealing, arose the childish voice, and the settler paused again, irresolute, and with deepening indignation. In his fancy he saw the steaming supper his wife would have awaiting him. He loathed the thought of retracing his steps, and then stumbling a quarter of a mile through the stumps and bog of the wood road. He was foot-sore as well as hungry, and he cursed the vagabond squatter with serious emphasis; but in that wailing was a terror which would not let him go on. He thought of his own little one left in such a position, and straightway his heart melted. He turned, dropped his bundle behind some

Do seek their meat from God

bushes, grasped his gun, and made speed back for the cabin.

"Who knows," he said to himself, "but that drunken idiot has left his youngster without a bite to eat in the whole miserable shanty? Or maybe he's locked out, and the poor little beggar's half scared to death. *Sounds* as if he was scared;" and at this thought the settler quickened his pace.

As the hungry panthers drew near the cabin, and the cries of the lonely child grew clearer, they hastened their steps, and their eyes opened to a wider circle, flaming with a greener fire. It would be thoughtless superstition to say the beasts were cruel. They were simply keen with hunger, and alive with the eager passion of the chase. They were not ferocious with any anticipation of battle, for they knew the voice was the voice of a child, and something in the voice told them the child was solitary.

Theirs was no hideous or unnatural *Do seek* rage, as it is the custom to describe *their meat* it. They were but seeking with the *from God* strength, the cunning, the deadly swiftness given them to that end, the food convenient for them. On their success in accomplishing that for which nature had so exquisitely designed them depended not only their own, but the lives of their blind and helpless young, now whimpering in the cave on the slope of the moon-lit ravine. They crept through a wet alder thicket, bounded lightly over the ragged brush fence, and paused to reconnoitre on the edge of the clearing, in the full glare of the moon. At the same moment the settler emerged from the darkness of the wood-road on the opposite side of the clearing. He saw the two great beasts, heads down and snouts thrust forward, gliding toward the open cabin door.

Do seek their meat from God   For a few moments the child had been silent. Now his voice rose again in pitiful appeal, a very ecstasy of loneliness and terror. There was a note in the cry that shook the settler's soul. He had a vision of his own boy, at home with his mother, safe-guarded from even the thought of peril. And here was this little one left to the wild beasts! "Thank God! Thank God I came!" murmured the settler, as he dropped on one knee to take a surer aim. There was a loud report (not like the sharp crack of a rifle), and the female panther, shot through the loins, fell in a heap, snarling furiously and striking with her fore-paws.

The male walked around her in fierce and anxious amazement. Presently, as the smoke lifted, he discerned the settler kneeling for a second shot. With a high screech of fury, the lithe brute sprang upon his enemy, taking a bullet full in his chest without seeming to know he *Do seek* was hit. Ere the man could slip in *their meat* another cartridge the beast was upon *from God* him, bearing him to the ground and fixing keen fangs in his shoulder. Without a word, the man set his strong fingers desperately into the brute's throat, wrenched himself partly free, and was struggling to rise, when the panther's body collapsed upon him all at once, a dead weight which he easily flung aside. The bullet had done its work just in time.

Quivering from the swift and dreadful contest, bleeding profusely from his mangled shoulder, the settler stepped up to the cabin door and peered in. He heard sobs in the darkness.

"Don't be scared, sonny," he said, in a reassuring voice. "I'm going to take you home along with me. Poor little lad, *I'll* look after you if folks that ought to don't."

Do seek their meat from God Out of the dark corner came a shout of delight, in a voice which made the settler's heart stand still. "*Daddy*, daddy," it said, "I *knew* you'd come. I was so frightened when it got dark!" And a little figure launched itself into the settler's arms, and clung to him trembling. The man sat down on the threshold and strained the child to his breast. He remembered how near he had been to disregarding the far-off cries, and great beads of sweat broke out upon his forehead.

Not many weeks afterwards the settler was following the fresh trail of a bear which had killed his sheep. The trail led him at last along the slope of a deep ravine, from whose bottom came the brawl of a swollen and obstructed stream. In the ravine he found a shallow cave, behind a great white rock. The cave was plainly a wild beast's lair, and he entered circumspectly. There were bones scattered about, and on some *Do seek* dry herbage in the deepest corner of *their meat* the den, he found the dead bodies, *from God* now rapidly decaying, of two small panther cubs.

Within Sound of the Saws.

Lumber had gone up, and the big mill on the Aspohegan was working overtime.

Through the range of square openings under the eaves the sunlight streamed in steadily upon the strident tumult, the confusion of sun and shadow, within the mill. The air was sweet with the smell of fresh sawdust and clammy with the ooze from great logs just "yanked" up the dripping slides from the river. One had to pitch his voice with peculiar care to make it audible amid the chaotic din of the saws.

In the middle of the mill worked the "gang," a series of upright saws that rose and fell swiftly, cleaving *Within* their way with a pulsating, vicious *Sound of* clamor through an endless and sullen *the Saws* procession of logs. Here and there, each with a massive table to itself, hummed the circulars, large and small; and whensoever a deal, or a pile of slabs, was brought in contact with one of the spinning discs, upon the first arching spirt of sawdust spray began a shrieking note, which would run the whole vibrant and intolerable gamut as the saw bit through the fibres from end to end. In the occasional brief moments of comparative silence, when several of the saws would chance to be disengaged at the same instant, might be heard, far down in the lower story of the mill, the grumbling roar of the two great turbine wheels, which, sucking in the tortured water from the sluices, gave life to all the wilderness of cranks and shafts above.

Within Sound of the Saws   That end of the mill which looked down river stood open, to a height of about seven feet, across the whole of the upper story. From this opening ran a couple of long slanting ways each two feet wide and about a hundred feet in length, raised on trestles. The track of these "slides," as they are technically termed, consisted of a series of wooden rollers, along which the deals raced in endless sequence from the saws, to drop with a plunge into a spacious basin, at the lower end of which they were gathered into rafts. Whenever there was a break in the procession of deals, the rollers would be left spinning briskly with a cheerful murmur. There was also a shorter and steeper "slide," diverging to the lumber yard, where clapboards and such light stuff were piled till they could be carted to the distant station.

In former days it had been the

easy custom to dump the sawdust *Within* into the stream, but the fish-wardens *Sound of* had lately interfered and put a stop *the Saws* to the practice. Now, a tall young fellow, in top boots, gray homespun trousers and blue shirt, was busy carting the sawdust to a swampy hollow near the lower end of the main slides.

Sandy MacPherson was a new hand. Only that morning had he joined the force at the Aspohegan Mill; and every now and then he would pause, remove his battered soft felt from his whitish yellow curls, mop his red forehead, and gaze with a hearty appreciation at the fair landscape spread out beyond the mill. With himself and with the world in general he felt on fairly good terms — an easy frame of mind which would have been much jarred had he been conscious of the fact that from a corner in the upper story of the mill his every movement was

Within Sound of the Saws watched with a vindictive and ominous interest.

In that corner, close by the head of one of the main slides, stood a table whose presiding genius was a little swinging circular. The circular was tended by a powerful, sombre-visaged old mill-hand called 'Lije Vandine, whose office it was to trim square the ragged ends of the "stuff" before it went down the slide. At the very back of the table hummed the saw, like a great hornet; and whenever Vandine got two or three deals in place before him he would grasp a lever above his head, and forward through its narrow slit in the table would dart the little saw, and scream its way in a second through the tough white spruce. Every time he let the saw swing back, Vandine would drop his eyes to the blue-shirted figure below, and his harsh features would work with concentrated fury. These seven years he had been waiting for the day when he should meet Sandy MacPherson face to face.

Within Sound of the Saws

Seven years before, 'Lije Vandine had been working in one of the mills near St. John, New Brunswick, while his only daughter, Sarah, was living out at service in the city. At this time Sandy MacPherson was employed on the city wharves, and an acquaintance which he formed with the pretty housemaid resulted in a promise of marriage between the two. Vandine and his wife were satisfied with the girl's account of her lover, and the months slipped by swiftly without their making his acquaintance. Among the fishing and lumbering classes, however, it not seldom happens that betrothal brings with it rather more intimate privileges than propriety could sanction, whence it came to pass that one evening Sarah returned to her parents unexpectedly, having been dismissed from her situation in disgrace. Vandine, though ignorant, was a clear-seeing man, who understood his own class thoroughly; and after his first outburst of wounded indignation he had forgiven and comforted his daughter no less tenderly than her mother had done. He knew perfectly that the girl was no wanton. He went at once into the city, with the intention of fetching Sandy out and covering up the disgrace by an immediate marriage. He visited the wharves, but the young man was not there. With growing apprehension he hastened to his boarding-house, only to learn that MacPherson had left the place and was departing for the States by the next train, having been married the previous evening. The man's pain and fury at this revelation almost choked him, but he mastered himself sufficiently to ask a boy of the house to accompany him to the station and point out the betrayer. If the *Within* train had not gone, he would be in *Sound of* time to avenge his poor girl. The *the Saws* boy, however, took alarm at something in Vandine's face, and led him by a roundabout way, so that just as he drew near the station the Western Express rolled out with increasing speed. On the rear platform stood a laughing young woman bedecked in many colors, and beside her a tall youth with a curly yellow head, whom the boy pointed out as Sandy MacPherson. He was beyond the reach of vengeance for the time. But his features stamped themselves ineffaceably on the avenger's memory. As the latter turned away, to bide his time in grim silence, the young woman on the platform of the car said to her husband, "I wonder who that was, Sandy, that looked like he was going to run after the cars! Did n't you see? His arms kind o' jerked out, like that; but he

Within Sound of the Saws did n't start after all. There he goes up the hill, with one pant-leg in his boot. He looked kind of wild. I 'm just as glad he did n't get aboard!"

"He 's one of your old fellers as you 've give the go-by to, I kind of suspicion, Sis," replied the young man with a laugh. And the train roared into a cutting.

About a year after these events Vandine's wife died, and Vandine thereupon removed, with Sarah and her baby, to the interior of the province, settling down finally at Aspohegan Mills. Here he built himself a small cottage, on a steep slope overlooking the mill; and here Sarah, by her quiet and self-sacrificing devotion to her father and her child, wiped out the memory of her error and won the warm esteem of the settlement. As for the child, he grew into a handsome, blue-eyed, sturdy boy, whom his grandfather loved with a passionate tenderness *Within* intensified by a subtle strain of pity. *Sound of* As year by year his daughter and *the Saws* the boy twined themselves ever closer about his heart, Vandine's hate against the man who had wronged them both kept ever deepening to a keener anguish.

But now at last the day had come. When first he had caught sight of MacPherson in the yard below, the impulse to rush down and throttle him was so tremendous that as he curbed it the blood forsook his face, leaving it the color of ashes, and for a few seconds he could not tend his saw. Presently, when the yelping little demon was again at work biting across the timbers, the foreman drew near, and Vandine asked him, "Who's the new hand down yonder?"

"Oh!" said the foreman, leaning a little over the bench to follow Vandine's pointing, "yon's one Sandy MacPherson, from over on

Within Sound of the Saws the Kennebec. He's been working in Maine these seven year past, but says he kind of got a hankering after his own country, an' so he's come back. Good hand!"

"*That* so!" was all Vandine replied.

All the long forenoon, amid the wild, or menacing, or warning, or complaining crescendos and diminuendos of the unresting saws, the man's brain seethed with plans of vengeance. After all these years of waiting he would be satisfied with no common retribution. To merely kill the betrayer would be insufficient. He would wring his soul and quench his manhood with some strange unheard-of horror, ere dealing the final stroke that should rid earth of his presence. Scheme after scheme burned through his mind, and at times his gaunt face would crease itself in a dreadful smile as he pulled the lever that drove his blade through the deals. Finding no plan altogether to his taste, however, he resolved to postpone his revenge till night, at least, that he might have the more time to think it over, and to indulge the luxury of anticipation with realization so easily within his grasp.

Within Sound of the Saws

At noon Vandine, muttering to himself, climbed the steep path to the little cottage on the hillside. He ate his dinner in silence, with apparently no perception of what was being set before him. His daughter dared not break in upon this preoccupation. Even his idolized Stevie could win from him no notice, save a smile of grim triumph that frightened the child. Just as he was leaving the cottage to return to the mill, he saw Sarah start back from the window and sit down suddenly, grasping at her bosom, and blanching to the lips as if she had seen a ghost. Glancing downward to the black road, deep with rotted

Within Sound of the Saws sawdust, he saw MacPherson passing.

"Who is it?" he asked the girl.

"It's Sandy," she murmured, flushing scarlet and averting her face.

Her father turned away without a word and started down the hill. Presently the girl remembered that there was something terrifying in the expression of his face as he asked the curt question. With a sudden vague fear rising in her breast, she ran to the cottage door.

"Father!" she cried, "father!" But Vandine paid no heed to her calls, and after a pause she turned back into the room to answer Stevie's demand for a cup of milk.

Along about the middle of the afternoon, while Sandy MacPherson was still carting sawdust, and Vandine tending his circular amid the bewildering din, Stevie and some other children came down to play *Within around the mill. Sound of*

The favorite amusement with these *the Saws* embryo mill-hands, stream-drivers, and lumbermen, was to get on the planks as they emerged from the upper story of the mill, and go careering swiftly and smoothly down the slides, till, just before coming to the final plunge, they would jump off, and fall on the heap of sawdust. This was a game that to strangers looked perilous enough; but there had never been an accident, so at Aspohegan Mills it had outgrown the disapproval of the hands. To Sandy MacPherson, however, it was new, and from time to time he eyed the sport apprehensively. And all the while Vandine glared upon him from his corner in the upper story, and the children raced shouting down the slides, and tumbled with bright laughter into the sawdust.

Among the children none enjoyed

Within Sound of the Saws more than Stevie this racing down the slides. His mother, looking out of the window on the hillside, saw the merry little figure, bareheaded, the long yellow curls floating out behind him, as he half knelt, half sat on the sliding plank ready to jump off at the proper moment. She had no thought of danger as she resumed her housework. Neither had Stevie. At length it happened, however, that just as he was nearing the end of the descent, an eagle came sailing low overhead, caught the little fellow's eye, and diverted his attention for a moment. It was the fatal moment. Just as he looked down again, gathering himself to jump, his heart sprang into his throat, and the plank with a sickening lurch plunged into the churning basin. The child's shrill, frightened shriek was not half uttered ere the waters choked it.

Vandine had just let the buzzing little circular slip back into its recess, when he saw MacPherson spring from *Within* his cart and dash madly down to the *Sound of the Saws* shore.

At the same instant came that shrill cry, so abruptly silenced. Vandine's heart stood still with awful terror, — he had recognized the child's voice. In a second he had swung himself down over the scaffolding, alighting on a sawdust heap.

"Hold back the deals!" he yelled in a voice that pierced the din. It was not five seconds ere every one in the mill seemed to know what had happened. Two men sprang on the slides and checked the stream of deals. Then the great turbines ceased to grumble, and all the clamor of the saws was hushed. The unexpected silence was like a blow, and sickened the nerves.

And meanwhile — Stevie? The plank that bore his weight clinging desperately to it, plunged deeper than its fellows, and came up some-

Within Sound of the Saws what further from the slide, but not now with Stevie upon it. The child had lost his hold, and when he rose it was only to strike against the bottoms of three or four deals that lay clustered together.

This, though apparently fatal, was in reality the child's salvation, for during the half or three-quarters of a minute that intervened before the slides could be stopped, the great planks kept dropping and plunging and crashing about him; and had it not been for those very timbers that cut him off from the air he was choking to breathe, he would have been crushed and battered out of all human semblance in a second. As it was, ere he had time to suffocate, MacPherson was on the spot.

In an instant the young man's heavy boots were kicked off, and without pausing to count the odds, which were hideously against him, he sprang into the chaos of whirling timbers. All about him pounded *Within* the falling deals, then ceased, just as *Sound of* he made a clean dive beneath that *the Saws* little cluster that covered Stevie. As Vandine reached the shore, and was casting desperate glances over the basin in search of some clue to guide his plunge, MacPherson reappeared at the other side of the deals, and Stevie's yellow curls were floating over his shoulder. The young man clung rather faintly to the supporting planks, as if he had overstrained himself; and two or three hands, who had already shoved off a "bateau," pushed out and picked him up with his burden.

Torn by a convulsion of fiercely antagonized passions, Vandine sat down on the edge of the bank and waited stupidly. About the same moment Sarah looked out of the cottage door in wonder to see why the mill had stopped so suddenly.

In all his dreams, Vandine had

[45]

Within Sound of the Saws never dreamed of such chance as that his enemy should deserve his gratitude. In his nature there had grown up one thing stronger than his thirst for vengeance, and that one thing was his love for Stevie. In spite of himself, and indeed to his furious self-scorn, he found his heart warming strangely to the man who, at deadliest risk, had saved the life of his darling. At the same time he was conscious of a fresh sense of injury. A bitter resentment throbbed up in his bewildered bosom, to think that MacPherson should thus have robbed him of the sweets of that revenge he had so long anticipated. The first clear realization that came to him was that, though he must kill the man who had wronged his girl, he would nevertheless be tortured with remorse for ever after. A moment more, and — as he saw Sandy step out of the " bateau " with the boy, now sobbing feebly, in his arms — he knew that his vengeance had been made for ever impossible. He longed fiercely to grasp the fellow's hand, and make some poor attempt to thank him. But he mastered the impulse — Sarah must not be forgotten. He strode down the bank. One of the hands had taken Stevie, and MacPherson was leaning against a pile of boards, panting for breath. Vandine stepped up to him, his fingers twitching, and struck him a furious blow across the mouth with his open hand. Then he turned aside, snatched Stevie to his bosom, and started up the bank. Before going two paces, however, he paused, as if oppressed by the utter stillness that followed his astounding act. Bending a strange look on the young man, he said, in a voice as harsh as the saw's: —

"I *was* going to kill you to-night, Sandy MacPherson. But now after this day's work of yourn, I guess yer

Within Sound of the Saws safe from me from this out." He shut his mouth with a snap, and strode up through the piles of sawdust toward the cottage on the hill.

As for MacPherson, he was dumbfounded. Though no boaster, he knew he had done a magnificently heroic thing, and to get his mouth slapped for it was an exigency which he did not know what to do with. He had staggered against the boards from the force of the stroke, but it had not occurred to him to resent it, though ordinarily he was hot-blooded and quick in a quarrel. He stared about him sheepishly, bewildered and abashed, and unspeakably aggrieved. In the faces of the mill-hands who were gathered about him, he found no solution of the mystery. They looked as astonished as himself, and almost equally hot and ashamed. Presently he ejaculated, "Well, I swan!" Then one of the men who had taken out the "bateau" and picked him up, found voice.

Within Sound of the Saws

"I'll be gosh-darned ef that ain't the damnedest," said he, slowly. "Why, so, I'd thought as how he was agoin' right down on his prayer-handles to ye. That there kid is the apple of his eye."

"An' he was sot on *killin'* me to-night, was he?" murmured Mac-Pherson in deepest wonderment. "What might his name be, anyhow?"

"'Lije Vandine," spoke up another of the hands. "An' that's his grandchild, Stevie. I reckon he must have a powerful grudge agin you, Sandy, or he'd never 'a' acted that way."

MacPherson's face had grown suddenly serious and dignified. "Is the boy's father and mother livin'?" he inquired.

"Sarah Vandine's living with the old man," answered the foreman,

[49]

Within Sound of the Saws " and as fine a girl as there'll be in Aspohegan. Don't know anything about the lad's father, nor don't want to. The man that'd treat a girl like Sarah Vandine that way — hangin's too good for 'im."

MacPherson's face flushed crimson, and he dropped his eyes.

" Boys," said he, huskily, " ef 'Lije Vandine had 'a' served me as he intended, I guess as how I'd have only got my deserts. I reckon as how *I'm* the little lad's father! "

The hands stared at each other. Nothing could make them forget what MacPherson had just done. They were all daring and ready in emergency, but each man felt that he would have thought twice before jumping into the basin when the deals were running on the slides. The foreman could have bitten his tongue out for what he had just said. He tried to mend matters.

" I wouldn't have thought you

was that sort of a man, to judge from what I've just seen o' you," he explained. "Anyhow, I reckon you've more 'n made up this day for the wrong you done when you was younger. But Sarah Vandine's as good a girl as they make, an' I don't hardly see how you could 'a' served her that trick."

A certain asperity grew in the foreman's voice as he thought of it; for, as his wife used to say, he "set a great store by 'Lije's girl, not havin' no daughter of his own."

"It was lies as done it, boys," said MacPherson. "As for *whose* lies, why *that* ain't neither here nor there, now — an' she as did the mischief's dead and buried — and before she died she told me all about it. That was last winter — of the grippe — and I tell you I've felt bad about Sarah ever since. An' to think the little lad's mine! *Boys,* but ain't

Within Sound of the Saws

he a beauty?" And Sandy's face began to beam with satisfaction at the thought.

By this time all the hands looked gratified at the turn affairs were, to them, so plainly taking. Every one returned to work, the foreman remarking aside to a chum, " I reckon Sarah's all right." And in a minute or two the saws were once more shrieking their way through the logs and slabs and deals.

On the following morning, as 'Lije Vandine tended his vicious little circular, he found its teeth needed resetting. They had been tried by a lot of knotty timber. He unshipped the saw and took it to the foreman. While he was waiting for the latter to get him another saw, Sandy MacPherson came up. With a strong effort Vandine restrained himself from holding out his hand in grateful greeting. There was a lull in the uproar, the men forgetting to feed their saws as they watched the interview. *Within Sound of the Saws*

Sandy's voice was heard all over the mill:—

"'Lije Vandine, I saved the little lad's life, an' *that* counts for *something*; but I know right well I ain't got no right to expect you or Sarah ever to say a kind word to me. But I swear, so help me God, I had n't no sort of idee what I was doin'. My wife died las' winter, over on the Kennebec, an' afore she died she told me everything — as I 'd take it kindly ef you 'd let *me* tell *you*, more particular, another time. An' as I was wantin' to say now, I 'd take it kind ef you 'd let me go up along to your place this evenin', and maybe Sarah 'd let me jest talk to the boy a little. Ef so be ez I could persuade her by-and-by to forget an' forgive — and you 'd trust me after what I 'd done — I 'd lay out to marry her the minute she 'd say the

Within Sound of the Saws word, fur there ain't no other woman I've ever set such store by as I do now by her. An' then ther's Stevie ——"

"Stevie and the lass hez both got a good home," interrupted Vandine, roughly.

"An' I would n't want a better for 'em," exclaimed MacPherson, eagerly, catching the train of the old man's thought. "What I'd want would be, ef maybe you'd let me come in along with them and you."

By this time Vandine had got his new saw, and he turned away without replying. Sandy followed him a few paces, and then turned back dejectedly to attend his own circular — he having been moved into the mill that morning. All the hands looked at him in sympathy, and many were the ingenious backwoods oaths which were muttered after Vandine for his ugliness. The old man paid little heed, however, to the tide of unpopularity that was rising *Within* about him. Probably, absorbed in *Sound of* his own thoughts, he was utterly un- *the Saws* aware of it. All the morning long he swung and fed his circular, and when the horn blew for twelve his mind was made up. In the sudden stillness he strode over to the place where MacPherson worked, and said in a voice of affected carelessness —

"You better come along an' have a bite o' dinner with us, Sandy. You'll be kinder expected, I reckon, for Stevie's powerful anxious to see you."

Sandy grabbed his coat and went along.

"The Young Ravens that Call upon Him."

It was just before dawn, and a grayness was beginning to trouble the dark about the top of the mountain.

Even at that cold height there was no wind. The veil of cloud that hid the stars hung but a hand-breadth above the naked summit. To eastward the peak broke away sheer, beetling in a perpetual menace to the valleys and the lower hills. Just under the brow, on a splintered and creviced ledge, was the nest of the eagles.

As the thick dark shrank down the steep like a receding tide, and the grayness reached the ragged heap of

"The Young Ravens that Call upon Him"

branches forming the nest, the young eagles stirred uneasily under the loose droop of the mother's wings. She raised her head and peered about her, slightly lifting her wings as she did so; and the nestlings, complaining at the chill air that came in upon their unfledged bodies, thrust themselves up amid the warm feathers of her thighs. The male bird, perched on a jutting fragment beside the nest, did not move. But he was awake. His white, narrow, flat-crowned head was turned to one side, and his yellow eye, under its straight, fierce lid, watched the pale streak that was growing along the distant eastern sea-line.

The great birds were racked with hunger. Even the nestlings, to meet the petitions of whose gaping beaks they stinted themselves without mercy, felt meagre and uncomforted. Day after day the parent birds had fished almost in vain; day after day

"The Young Ravens that Call upon Him" their wide and tireless hunting had brought them scant reward. The schools of alewives, mackerel, and herring seemed to shun their shores that spring. The rabbits seemed to have fled from all the coverts about their mountain.

The mother eagle, larger and of mightier wing than her mate, looked as if she had met with misadventure. Her plumage was disordered. Her eyes, fiercely and restlessly anxious, at moments grew dull as if with exhaustion. On the day before, while circling at her viewless height above a lake far inland, she had marked a huge lake-trout, basking near the surface of the water. Dropping upon it with half-closed, hissing wings, she had fixed her talons in its back. But the fish had proved too powerful for her. Again and again it had dragged her under water, and she had been almost drowned before she could unloose the terrible grip of her claws. Hardly, and late, had she beaten her way back to the mountain-top.

And now the pale streak in the east grew ruddy. Rust-red stains and purple, crawling fissures began to show on the rocky face of the peak. A piece of scarlet cloth, woven among the fagots of the nest, glowed like new blood in the increasing light. And presently a wave of rose appeared to break and wash down over the summit, as the rim of the sun came above the horizon.

The male eagle stretched his head far out over the depth, lifted his wings and screamed harshly, as if in greeting of the day. He paused a moment in that position, rolling his eye upon the nest. Then his head went lower, his wings spread wider, and he launched himself smoothly and swiftly into the abyss of air as a swimmer glides into the sea. The female watched him, a faint wraith

"The Young Ravens that Call upon Him" of a bird darting through the gloom, till presently, completing his mighty arc, he rose again into the full light of the morning. Then on level, all but moveless wing, he sailed away toward the horizon.

As the sun rose higher and higher, the darkness began to melt on the tops of the lower hills and to diminish on the slopes of the upland pastures, lingering in the valleys as the snow delays there in spring. As point by point the landscape uncovered itself to his view, the eagle shaped his flight into a vast circle, or rather into a series of stupendous loops. His neck was stretched toward the earth, in the intensity of his search for something to ease the bitter hunger of his nestlings and his mate.

Not far from the sea, and still in darkness, stood a low, round hill, or swelling upland. Bleak and shelterless, whipped by every wind that the heavens could let loose, it bore no bush but an occasional juniper scrub. It was covered with mossy hillocks, and with a short grass, meagre but sweet. There in the chilly gloom, straining her ears to catch the lightest footfall of approaching peril, but hearing only the hushed thunder of the surf, stood a lonely ewe over the lamb to which she had given birth in the night.

"The Young Ravens that Call upon Him"

Having lost the flock when the pangs of travail came upon her, the unwonted solitude filled her with apprehension. But as soon as the first feeble bleating of the lamb fell upon her ear, everything was changed. Her terrors all at once increased tenfold, — but they were for her young, not for herself; and with them came a strange boldness such as her heart had never known before. As the little weakling shivered against her side, she uttered low, short bleats and murmurs of tenderness. When

"The Young Ravens that Call upon Him" an owl hooted in the woods across the valley, she raised her head angrily and faced the sound, suspecting a menace to her young. When a mouse scurried past her, with a small, rustling noise amid the withered mosses of the hillock, she stamped fiercely, and would have charged had the intruder been a lion.

When the first gray of dawn descended over the pasture, the ewe feasted her eyes with the sight of the trembling little creature, as it lay on the wet grass. With gentle nose she coaxed it and caressed it, till presently it struggled to its feet, and, with its pathetically awkward legs spread wide apart to preserve its balance, it began to nurse. Turning her head as far around as she could, the ewe watched its every motion with soft murmurings of delight.

And now that wave of rose, which had long ago washed the mountain and waked the eagles, spread tenderly

across the open pasture. The lamb
stopped nursing; and the ewe, moving forward two or three steps, tried
to persuade it to follow her. She
was anxious that it should as soon
as possible learn to walk freely, so
they might together rejoin the flock.
She felt that the open pasture was
full of dangers.

"The Young Ravens that Call upon Him"

The lamb seemed afraid to take so
many steps. It shook its ears and
bleated piteously. The mother returned to its side, caressed it anew,
pushed it with her nose, and again
moved away a few feet, urging it to
go with her. Again the feeble little
creature refused, bleating loudly.
At this moment there came a terrible hissing rush out of the sky,
and a great form fell upon the lamb.
The ewe wheeled and charged madly;
but at the same instant the eagle,
with two mighty buffetings of his
wings, rose beyond her reach and

"The Young Ravens that Call upon Him" soared away toward the mountain. The lamb hung limp from his talons; and with piteous cries the ewe ran beneath, gazing upward, and stumbling over the hillocks and juniper bushes.

In the nest of the eagles there was content. The pain of their hunger appeased, the nestlings lay dozing in the sun, the neck of one resting across the back of the other. The triumphant male sat erect upon his perch, staring out over the splendid world that displayed itself beneath him. Now and again he half lifted his wings and screamed joyously at the sun. The mother bird, perched upon a limb on the edge of the nest, busily rearranged her plumage. At times she stooped her head into the nest to utter over her sleeping eaglets a soft chuckling noise, which seemed to come from the bottom of her throat.

"THE LAMB HUNG LIMP FROM HIS TALONS."

But hither and thither over the round bleak hill wandered the ewe, calling for her lamb, unmindful of the flock, which had been moved to other pastures.

"The Young Ravens that Call upon Him"

Strayed.

In the Cabineau Camp, of unlucky reputation, there was a young ox of splendid build, but of a wild and restless nature.

He was one of a yoke, of part Devon blood, large, dark-red, all muscle and nerve, and with wide magnificent horns. His yoke-fellow was a docile steady worker, the pride of his owner's heart; but he himself seemed never to have been more than half broken in. The woods appeared to draw him by some spell. He wanted to get back to the pastures where he had roamed untrammelled of old with his fellow-steers. The remembrance was in his heart

of the dewy mornings when the herd *Strayed*
used to feed together on the sweet
grassy hillocks, and of the clover-
smelling heats of June when they
would gather hock-deep in the pools
under the green willow-shadows.
He hated the yoke, he hated the
winter; and he imagined that in the
wild pastures he remembered it
would be for ever summer. If only
he could get back to those pastures!

One day there came the longed-for
opportunity; and he seized it. He
was standing unyoked beside his
mate, and none of the teamsters
were near. His head went up in
the air, and with a snort of triumph
he dashed away through the forest.

For a little while there was a vain
pursuit. At last the lumbermen
gave it up. "Let him be!" said
his owner, "an' I rayther guess he'll
turn up agin when he gits peckish.
He kaint browse on spruce buds an'
lung-wort."

Strayed Plunging on with long gallop through the snow he was soon miles from camp. Growing weary he slackened his pace. He came down to a walk. As the lonely red of the winter sunset began to stream through the openings of the forest, flushing the snows of the tiny glades and swales, he grew hungry, and began to swallow unsatisfying mouthfuls of the long moss which roughened the tree-trunks. Ere the moon got up he had filled himself with this fodder, and then he lay down in a little thicket for the night.

But some miles back from his retreat a bear had chanced upon his foot-prints. A strayed steer! That would be an easy prey. The bear started straightway in pursuit. The moon was high in heaven when the crouched ox heard his pursuer's approach. He had no idea what was coming, but he rose to his feet and waited.

The bear plunged boldly into the *Strayed* thicket, never dreaming of resistance. With a muffled roar the ox charged upon him and bore him to the ground. Then he wheeled, and charged again, and the astonished bear was beaten at once. Gored by those keen horns he had no stomach for further encounter, and would fain have made his escape; but as he retreated the ox charged him again, dashing him against a huge trunk. The bear dragged himself up with difficulty, beyond his opponent's reach; and the ox turned scornfully back to his lair.

At the first yellow of dawn the restless creature was again upon the march. He pulled more mosses by the way, but he disliked them the more intensely now because he thought he must be nearing his ancient pastures with their tender grass and their streams. The snow was deeper about him, and his hatred of the

Strayed winter grew apace. He came out upon a hill-side, partly open, whence the pine had years before been stripped, and where now grew young birches thick together. Here he browsed on the aromatic twigs, but for him it was harsh fare.

As his hunger increased he thought a little longingly of the camp he had deserted, but he dreamed not of turning back. He would keep on till he reached his pastures, and the glad herd of his comrades licking salt out of the trough beside the accustomed pool. He had some blind instinct as to his direction, and kept his course to the south very strictly, the desire in his heart continually leading him aright.

That afternoon he was attacked by a panther, which dropped out of a tree and tore his throat. He dashed under a low branch and scraped his assailant off, then, wheeling about savagely, put the brute to flight with his first mad charge. The panther sprang back into his tree, and the ox continued his quest.

Soon his steps grew weaker, for the panther's cruel claws had gone deep into his neck, and his path was marked with blood. Yet the dream in his great wild eyes was not dimmed as his strength ebbed away. His weakness he never noticed or heeded. The desire that was urging him absorbed all other thoughts, —even, almost, his sense of hunger. This, however, it was easy for him to assuage, after a fashion, for the long, gray, unnourishing mosses were abundant.

By and by his path led him into the bed of a stream, whose waters could be heard faintly tinkling on thin pebbles beneath their coverlet of ice and snow. His slow steps conducted him far along this open course. Soon after he had disappeared, around a curve in the dis-

Strayed tance there came the panther, following stealthily upon his crimsoned trail. The crafty beast was waiting till the bleeding and the hunger should do its work, and the object of its inexorable pursuit should have no more heart left for resistance.

This was late in the afternoon. The ox was now possessed with his desire, and would not lie down for any rest. All night long, through the gleaming silver of the open spaces, through the weird and checkered gloom of the deep forest, heedless even of his hunger, or perhaps driven the more by it as he thought of the wild clover bunches and tender timothy awaiting him, the solitary ox strove on. And all night, lagging far behind in his unabating caution, the panther followed him.

At sunrise the worn and stumbling animal came out upon the borders of the great lake, stretching its leagues of unshadowed snow away to the south before him. There was his *Strayed* path, and without hesitation he followed it. The wide and frost-bound water here and there had been swept clear of its snows by the wind, but for the most part its covering lay unruffled; and the pale dove-colors, and saffrons, and rose-lilacs of the dawn were sweetly reflected on its surface.

The doomed ox was now journeying very slowly, and with the greatest labor. He staggered at every step, and his beautiful head drooped almost to the snow. When he had got a great way out upon the lake, at the forest's edge appeared the pursuing panther, emerging cautiously from the coverts. The round tawny face and malignant green eyes were raised to peer out across the expanse. The laboring progress of the ox was promptly marked. Dropping its nose again to the ensanguined snow, the beast resumed his pursuit, first

Strayed at a slow trot, and then at a long, elastic gallop. By this time the ox's quest was nearly done. He plunged forward upon his knees, rose again with difficulty, stood still, and looked around him. His eyes were clouding over, but he saw, dimly, the tawny brute that was now hard upon his steps. Back came a flash of the old courage, and he turned, horns lowered, to face the attack. With the last of his strength he charged, and the panther paused irresolutely; but the wanderer's knees gave way beneath his own impetus, and his horns ploughed the snow. With a deep bellowing groan he rolled over on his side, and the longing, and the dream of the pleasant pastures, faded from his eyes. With a great spring the panther was upon him, and the eager teeth were at his throat, — but he knew nought of it. No wild beast, but his own desire, had conquered him.

"HE SAW, DIMLY, THE TAWNY BRUTE."

When the panther had slaked his *Strayed*
thirst for blood, he raised his head,
and stood with his fore-paws resting
on the dead ox's side, and gazed all
about him.

To one watching from the lake
shore, had there been any one to
watch in that solitude, the wild beast
and his prey would have seemed but
a speck of black on the gleaming
waste. At the same hour, league
upon league back in the depth of the
ancient forest, a lonely ox was low-
ing in his stanchions, restless, refus-
ing to eat, grieving for the absence
of his yoke-fellow.

The Butt of the Camp.

He was a mean-looking specimen, this Simon Gillsey, and the Gornish Camp was not proud of him. His neck was long, his mouth was long and protruding, like a bird's beak, his hair was thin and colorless, his shoulders sloped in such a manner that his arms, which were long and lean, seemed to start from somewhere near his waist.

His body started forward from the hips, and he used his hands in a deprecating fashion that seemed to beseech so much recognition as might be conveyed in a passing kick.

He was muscular to a degree that would never be guessed from his make-up, but the camp was possessed with a sense of shame at tolerating his presence, and protected its self-respect by reminding him continually that he was considered beneath contempt.

Simon seemed quite unconscious of the difference between the truth and a lie. It was not that he lied from malice — the hands said he had n't "spunk" enough to know what malice was — but sheer mental obliquity led him to lie by preference, unless he saw reason to believe that the truth would conciliate his comrades.

He used to steal tobacco and other trifles whenever he found a good opportunity, and when he was caught his repentance was that of fear rather than of shame.

At the same time, the poor wretch was thoroughly courageous in the face of some physical and external dangers. The puniest man in camp could cow him with a look, yet none

The Butt of the Camp was prompter than he to face the grave perils of breaking a log-jam, and there was no cooler hand than his in the risky labors of stream-driving. Altogether he was a disagreeable problem to the lumbermen, who resented any element of pluck in one so unmanly and meagre-spirited as he was.

In spite of their contempt, however, they could ill have done without this cringing axeman. He did small menial services for his fellows, was ordered about at all times uncomplainingly, and bore the blame for everything that went wrong in the Gornish Camp.

When one of the hands was in a particularly bad humor, he could always find some relief for his feelings by kicking Gillsey in the shins, at which Gillsey would but smile an uneasy protest, showing the conspicuous absence of his upper front teeth.

Then again the Gornish Camp was waggishly inclined. The hands were much addicted to practical jokes. It was not always wholesome to play these on each other, but Gillsey afforded a safe object for the ingenuity of the backwoods wit. *The Butt of the Camp*

For instance, whenever the men thought it was time to "chop a fellow down," in default of a greenhorn from the older settlements they would select Gillsey for the victim, and order that reluctant scarecrow up to the tree-top. This was much like the hunting of a tame fox, as far as exhilaration and manliness were concerned; but sport is sport, and the men would have their fun, with the heedless brutality of primitive natures.

This diversion, though rough and dangerous, is never practised on any but green hands or unwary visitors; but all signs fail in dry weather, and for Gillsey no traditions held.

The Butt of the Camp When he had climbed as high as his tormentors thought advisable — which usually was just as high as the top of the tree — a couple of vigorous choppers would immediately attack the tree with their axes.

As the tall trunk began to topple with a sickening hesitation, Gillsey's eyes would stick out and his thin hair seem to stand on end, for to this torture he never grew accustomed. Then, as the men yelled with delight, the mass of dark branches would sweep down with a soft, windy crash into the snow, and Gillsey, pale and nervous, but adorned with that unfailing toothless smile, would pick himself out of the *débris* and slink off to camp.

The men usually consoled him after such an experience with a couple of plugs of "black-jack" tobacco, — which seemed to him ample compensation.

In camp at night, when the hands *The Butt* had all gone to bed, two or three *of the* wakeful ones would sometimes get *Camp* up to have a smoke in the firelight. Such a proceeding almost always resulted in skylarking, of which Simon would be the miserable object. Perhaps the arch-conspirator would go to the cook's flour-barrel, fill his mouth with dry flour, and then, climbing to the slumbering Simon's bunk, would blow the dusty stuff in a soft, thin stream all over the sleeper's face and hair and scraggy beard. This process was called "blowing him," and was counted a huge diversion.

On soft nights, when the camp was hot and damp, it made, of course, a sufficiently nasty mess in the victim's hair, but Gillsey, by contrast, seemed rather to enjoy it. It never woke him up.

If the joker's mood happened to be more boisterous, the approved

The Butt of the Camp procedure was to softly uncover Gillsey's feet, and tie a long bit of salmon twine to each big toe. After waking all the other hands, the conspirators would retire to their bunks.

Presently some one would give a smart tug on one of the strings, and pass it over hastily to his neighbor. Gillsey would wake up with a nervous yell, and grabbing his toe, seek to extricate it from the loop. Then would come another and sharper pull at the other toe, diverting Gillsey's attention to that member.

The game would be kept up till the bunks were screaming with laughter, and poor Gillsey bathed in perspiration and anxiety. Then the boss would interfere, and Gillsey would be set free.

These are only instances of what the butt was made to endure, though he was probably able to thrash almost any one of his tormentors, and had he mustered spirit to attempt this, all the camp would have seen that he got fair play.

The Butt of the Camp

At last, however, it began to be suspected that Gillsey was stealing from the pork barrels and other stores. This was serious, and the men would not play any more jokes upon the culprit. Pending proof, he was left severely to himself, and enjoyed comparative peace for nearly a week.

This peace, strange to say, did not seem to please him. The strange creature hated to be ignored, and even courted further indignities. No one would notice him, however, till one night when he came in late, and undertook to sleep on the "deacon-seat."

A word of explanation is needed here. The "deacon-seat" — why so called I cannot say — is a raised platform running alongside of the stove, between the chimney and the tier of bunks. It is, of course, a splendid place to sleep on a bitter night, but no one is allowed so to occupy it, because in that position he shuts off the warmth from the rest.

The hands were all apparently asleep when Gillsey, after a long solitary smoke, reached for his blanket, and rolled himself up on the coveted "deacon-seat," with his back to the glowing fire. After a deprecating grin directed toward the silent bunks, he sank to sleep.

Soon in the bunks arose a whispered consultation, as a result of which stalwart woodsmen climbed down, braced their backs against the lower tier, doubled up their knees, and laid their sock feet softly against the sleeper's form. At a given signal the legs all straightened out with tremendous force, and poor Gillsey shot right across the "deacon-seat" and brought up with a thud upon the stove.

With a yell, he bounced away from his scorching quarters and plunged into his bunk, not burnt, but very badly scared. After that he eschewed the "deacon-seat."

The Butt of the Camp

At last the unfortunate wretch was caught purloining the pork. It became known in the camp, somehow, that he was a married man, and father of a family as miserable and shiftless as himself. Here was an explanation of his raids upon the provisions, for nobody in the camp would for a moment imagine that Gillsey could, unaided, support a family.

One Sunday night he was tracked to a hollow about a mile from camp, where he was met by a gaunt, wild, eccentric-looking girl, who was clearly his daughter. The two proceeded to an old stump concealed under some logs in a thicket, and out of the hollow of the stump Gillsey fished a lump of salt pork, together with a big bundle of "hard-tack," and a

The Butt of the Camp parcel or two of some other kind of provender.

The girl threw herself upon the food like a famishing animal, devoured huge mouthfuls, and then, gathering all promiscuously into her scanty skirt, darted off alone through the gloom. As soon as she had disappeared with her stores, Gillsey was captured and dragged back to camp.

At first he was too helpless with terror to open his mouth; but when formally arraigned before the boss he found his tongue. He implored forgiveness in the most piteous tones, while at the same time he flatly denied every charge. He even declared he was not married, that he had no family, and that he knew no one at all in the Gornish district or that part of the province.

But the boss knew all about him, even to his parentage. He lived about ten miles from the camp, across the mountains, on the Gornish River itself. As for his guilt, there was no room for a shadow of uncertainty.

The Butt of the Camp

A misdemeanor of this sort is always severely handled in the lumber camps. But every man, from the boss down, was filled with profound compassion for Gillsey's family. A family so afflicted as to own Gillsey for husband and sire appeared to them deserving of the tenderest pity.

It was the pathetic savagery and haggardness of the young girl that had moved the woodmen to let her off with her booty; and now, the boss declared, if Gillsey were dismissed without his wages — as was customary, in addition to other punishment — the family would surely starve, cut off from the camp pork-barrel. It was decided to give the culprit his wages up to date. Then came the rough-and-ready sentence of the camp-followers. The prisoner

The Butt of the Camp was to be "dragged" — the most humiliating punishment on the woodmen's code.

Gillsey's tears of fright were of no avail. He was wrapped in a sort of winding-sheet of canvas, smeared from head to foot with grease to make him slip smoothly, and hitched by the fettered wrists to a pair of horses. The strange team was then driven, at a moderate pace, for about half a mile along the main wood-road, the whole camp following in procession, and jeering at the unhappy thief.

When the man was unhitched, unbound, and set upon his feet, — not physically the worse for his punishment save that, presumably, his wrists ached somewhat, — he was given a bundle containing his scanty belongings, and told to "streak" for home. As he seemed reluctant to obey, he was kicked into something like alacrity.

When he had got well out of sight the woodmen returned to their camp. As for the wretched Gillsey, after the lamentations wherewith he enlivened his tramp had sunk to silence, he began to think his bundle remarkably heavy. He sat down on a stump to examine it. To his blank amazement he found a large lump of pork and a small bag of flour wrapped up in his dilapidated overalls.

The Butt of the Camp

The snow was unusually deep in the woods that winter, and toward spring there came a sudden, prolonged, and heavy thaw. The ice broke rapidly and every loosened brook became a torrent. Past the door of the camp, which was set in a valley, the Gornish River went boiling and roaring like a mill-race, all-forgetful of its wonted serene placidity.

From the camp to Gillsey's wretched cabin was only about ten miles across the mountain, but by the

The Butt of the Camp stream, which made a great circuit to get around a spur of the hills, it was hardly less than three times as far.

To Gillsey, in his log hut on a lofty knoll by the stream, the winter had gone by rather happily. The degradation of his punishment hardly touched him or his barbarous brood; and his wages had brought him food enough to keep the wolf from the door. He had nothing to do but to sit in his cabin and watch the approach of spring, while his lean boys snared an occasional rabbit.

At last, on a soft moonlight night, when the woods were full of the sounds of melting and settling snow, a far-off, ominous roaring smote his ear and turned his gaze down to the valley. Down the stream, on the still night, came the deadly, rushing sound, momently increasing in volume. The tall girl, she who had carried off the pork, heard the noise, and came to her father's side.

"Hackett's dam's bust, shore!" she exclaimed in a moment.

Gillsey turned upon her one of his deprecating, toothless smiles. "'T aint a-goin' ter tech us here," said he; "but I'm powerful glad ter be outer the Gornish Camp ter night. Them chaps be a-goin' ter ketch it, blame the'r skins!"

The girl — she was a mere overgrown child of fourteen or fifteen — looked thoughtful a moment, and then darted toward the woods.

"Whar yer goin', sis?" called Gillsey, in a startled voice.

"Warn 'em!" said the girl, laconically, not stopping her pace.

"Stop! stop! Come back!" shouted her father, starting in pursuit. But the girl never paused.

"Blame the'r skins! Blame the'r skins!" murmured Gillsey to himself. Then, seeing that he was not gaining on the child, he seemed to gulp something down in his throat, and finally he shouted: —

"*I'll* go, sis, *honest* I'll go. Yer kaint do it yerself. Come back home!"

The girl stopped, turned round, and walked back, saying to her father, "They 've kep' us the winter. Yer *must* git thar in time, dad!"

Gillsey went by the child, at a long trot, without answering, and disappeared in the woods; and at the same moment the flood went through the valley, filling it half-way up to the spot where the cabin stood.

That lanky youngster's word was law to the father, and she had set his thoughts in a new channel. He felt the camp must be saved, if he died for it. The girl said so. He only remembered now how easily the men had let him off, when they might have half-killed him; and their jests and jeers and tormentings he forgot.

His loose-hung frame gave him a *The Butt* long stride, and his endurance was *of the* marvellous. Through the gray and *Camp* silver glades, over stumps and windfalls, through thickets and black valleys and treacherous swamps, he went leaping at almost full speed.

Before long the tremendous effort began to tell. At first he would not yield; but presently he realized that he was in danger of giving out, so he slackened speed a little, in order to save his powers. But as he came out upon the valley and neared the camp, he caught once more a whisper of the flood, and sprang forward desperately. Could he get there in time? The child had said he *must*. He *would*.

His mouth was dry as a board, and he gasped painfully for breath, as he stumbled against the campdoor; and the roar of the flood was in his ears. Unable to speak at first, he battered furiously on the door

The Butt of the Camp with an axe, and then smashed in the window.

As the men came jumping wrathfully from their bunks, he found voice to yell:—

"The water! Dam broke! Run! Run!"

But the noise of the onrushing flood was now in their startled ears, and they needed no words to tell them their awful peril. Not staying an instant, every man ran for the hillside, barefooted in the snow. Ere they reached a safe height, Gillsey stumbled and fell, utterly exhausted, and for a moment no one noticed his absence.

Then the boss of the camp looked back and saw him lying motionless in his tracks. Already the camp had gone down under the torrent, and the flood was about to lick up the prostrate figure; but the boss turned back with tremendous bounds, swung Gillsey over his shoulder like a sack of oats, and staggered up the slope, as the water swelled, with a sobbing moan, from his ankles to his knees.

The Butt of the Camp

Seeing the situation of the boss, several more of the hands, who had climbed to a level of safety, rushed to the rescue. They seized him and his burden, while others formed a chain, laying hold of hands. With a shout the whole gang surged up the hill, — and the river saw its prey dragged out of its very teeth.

After a rest of a few moments, Gillsey quite recovered, and began most abject apologies for not getting to camp sooner, so as to give the boys time to save something.

The demonstrative hand-shakings and praises and gratitude of the men whom he had snatched from a frightful death seemed to confuse him. He took it at first for chaff, and said, humbly, that "Bein' as sis wanted him to git thar in time, he'd did his best." But at length it dawned upon him that his comrades regarded him as a man, as a hero, who had done a really splendid and noble thing. He began to feel their gratitude and their respect.

Then it seemed as if a transformation was worked upon the poor cringing fellow, and he began to believe in himself. A new, firmer, manlier light woke in his eye, and he held himself erect. He presently began to move about among the woodsmen as their equal, and their enduring gratitude gave his new self-confidence time to ripen. From that day Simon Gillsey stood on a higher plane. In that one act of heroism he had found his slumbering manhood.

At the Rough-and-Tumble Landing.

The soft smell of thawing snow was in the air, proclaiming April to the senses of the lumbermen as unmistakably as could any calendar.

The ice had gone out of the Big Aspohegan with a rush. There was an air of expectation about the camp. Everything was ready for a start down-stream. The hands who had all winter been chopping and hauling in the deep woods were about to begin the more toilsome and perilous task of "driving" the logs down the swollen river to the great booms and unresting mills about its

At the Rough-and-Tumble Landing mouth. One thing only remained to be done ere the drive could get under way. The huge "brow" of logs overhanging the stream had yet to be released. To whom would fall the task of accomplishing its release, was a question still undecided.

The perils of "stream-driving" on a bad river have been dwelt upon, I suppose, by every writer who has occupied his pen at all with the life of the lumber-camps. But to the daring backwoodsman there seldom falls a task more hazardous than that of cutting loose a brow of logs when the logs have been piled in the form of what is called a "rough-and-tumble landing." Such a landing is constructed by driving long timbers into the mud at the water's edge, below a steep piece of bank. Along the inner side of these are laid horizontally a certain number of logs, to form a water front; and into the space behind are tumbled helter-skelter from the tops of the bank the logs of the winter's chopping. It is a very simple and expeditious way of storing the logs. But when the ice has run out, and it is time to start the lumber down-stream, then comes trouble. The piles sustaining the whole vast weight of the brow have to be cut away, and the problem that confronts the chopper is how to escape the terrific rush of the falling logs.

At the Rough-and-Tumble Landing

Hughey McElvey, the boss of the Aspohegan camp, swinging an axe (rather as a badge of office than because he thought he might want to chop anything), sauntered down to the water's edge and took a final official glance at the brow of logs. Its foundations had been laid while McElvey was down with a touch of fever, and he was ill satisfied with them. For perhaps the fiftieth time, he shook his head and grumbled, "It's goin' to be a resky job gittin'

At the Rough-and-Tumble Landing

them logs clear." Then he rejoined the little cluster of men on top of the bank.

As he did so, a tall girl with splendid red hair came out of the camp and stepped up to his side. This was Laurette, the boss's only daughter, who had that morning driven over from the settlements in the back country, to bring him some comforts of mended woollens and to bid "the drive" God-speed. From McElvey the girl inherited her vivid hair and her superb proportions; and from her mother, who had been one Laurette Beaulieu, of Grande Anse, she got her mirthful black eyes and her smooth, dusky complexion, which formed so striking a contrast to her radiant tresses. A little conscious of all the eyes that centred upon her with varying degrees of admiration, love, desire, or self-abasing devotion, she felt the soft color deepen in her cheeks as she playfully took possession of McElvey's axe.

"*You 're* not goin' to do it, father, I reckon!" she exclaimed.

"No, sis," answered the boss, smiling down at her, "leastways, not unless the hands is all scared."

"Well, who *is* goin' to?" she inquired, letting her glance sweep rapidly over the stalwart forms that surrounded her. A shrewd observer might have noted that her eyes shyly avoided one figure, that stood a little apart from the rest, — the figure of a strongly-built man of medium size, who looked small among his large-moulded fellows. As for Jim Reddin, who was watching the girl's every movement, his heart tightened with a bitter pang as her eyes thus seemed to pass him over. Having, for all his forty years, a plentiful lack of knowledge of the feminine heart and its methods, he imagined himself ignored. And

At the Rough-and-Tumble Landing yet had he not Laurette's promise that none other than he should have the privilege of driving her home to the settlements that afternoon?

"That's what we're just a-goin' to decide," said McElvey, in answer to Laurette's question. "But first," he continued, with a sly chuckle, "had n't you better pick out the feller that's goin' to drive you home, sis? We're goin' to be powerful well occupied, all hands, when we git a start on them logs, I tell you!"

At this suggestion a huge young woodsman who was standing behind some of the others, out of Laurette's range of vision, started eagerly forward. Bill Goodine was acknowledged to be the best-looking man on the Big Aspohegan, — an opinion in which he himself most heartily concurred. He was also noted as a wrestler and fighter. He was an ardent admirer of Laurette; but his passion had not taught him any humility, and he felt confident that in order to gain the coveted honor of driving the girl home he had nothing to do but apply for it. He felt that it would hardly be the "square thing" to put Laurette to the embarrassment of inviting him right there before all the hands. Before he could catch her eye, however, Laurette had spoken what surely the devil of coquetry must have whispered in her ear. Undoubtedly, she had promised Jim Reddin that he should drive her home. But "let him show that he appreciates the favor," she thought to herself; and aloud, with a toss of her head, she exclaimed, "I'll take the one that cuts out the logs, — if he wants to come!"

The effect of this speech was instantaneous. Fully half the hands stepped forward, exclaiming, "I'll do it! — I'll do it, boss! — I'm your man, Mr. McElvey!" But Bill Goodine sprang to the front with a vigor that brushed aside all in his path. Thrusting himself in front of the laughing McElvey, he shouted, "I spoke first! I claim the job!" And, snatching up an axe, he started down the bank.

"Hold on!" shouted McElvey; but Goodine paid no attention. "Come back, I tell you!" roared the boss. "The job's yours, so hold on!" Upon this Bill came swaggering back, and gazed about him triumphantly.

"I guess *I'm* your teamster, eh, Laurette?" he murmured. But, to his astonishment, Laurette did not seem to hear him. She was casting quick glances of anger and disappointment in the direction of Jim Reddin, who leaned on a sled-stake and appeared to take no interest in the proceedings. Goodine flushed with jealous wrath, and was about to fling some gibe at Reddin, when McElvey remarked, —

"That's all very well, sis; and it has kinder simplified matters a lot. But I'm thinkin' you'd better have another one of the boys to fall back on. This 'ere's an onusual ticklish job; and the feller as does it'll be lucky if he comes off with a whole skin."

At these words so plain an expression of relief went over Laurette's face that Bill Goodine could not contain himself.

"Jim Reddin *dasn't* do it," he muttered to her, fiercely.

The girl drew herself up. "I never said he dast," she replied. "An' what's Jim Reddin to me, I'd like to know?" And then, being furious at Jim, at herself, and at Goodine, she was on the point of telling the latter that *he* shouldn't drive her home, anyway, when she reflected that this would excite com-

At the Rough-and-Tumble Landing ment, and restrained herself. But Reddin, who imagined that the whole thing was a scheme on Laurette's part for getting out of her promise to him, and who felt, consequently, as if the heavens were falling about his ears, had caught Goodine's mention of his name. He stepped up and asked sharply, "What's that about Jim Reddin?"

Laurette was gazing at him in a way that pierced his jealous pain and and thrilled his heart strangely; and as he looked at her he began to forget Bill Goodine altogether. But Goodine was not to be forgotten.

"I said," he cried, in a loud voice, "that you, Jim Reddin, jest *das n't* cut out them logs. You think yourself some punkins, you do; but ye're a coward!" And, swinging his great form round insolently, Goodine picked up his axe and sauntered down the bank.

Now, Laurette, as well as most of

the hands, looked to see this insult *At the* promptly resented in the only way *Rough-* consistent with honor. Reddin, *and-* though tender-hearted and slow to *Tumble* anger, was regarded as being, with *Landing* the possible exception of Goodine, the strongest man in that section of the country. He had proved his daring by many a bold feat in the rapids and the jams ; and his prowess as a fighter had been displayed more than once when a backwoods bully required a thrashing. But now he gave the Aspohegan camp a genuine surprise. First, the blood left his face, his eyes grew small and piercing, and his hands clenched spasmodically as he took a couple of steps after Goodine's retreating figure. Then his face flushed scarlet, and he turned to Laurette with a look of absolutely piteous appeal.

"I *can't* fight him," he tried to explain, huskily. "You don't understand. I ain't *afeard* of him,

At the Rough-and-Tumble Landing

nor of any man. But I vowed to his mother I'd be good to the lad, and —"

"Oh, I reckon I quite understand, Mr. Reddin," interrupted the girl, in a hard, clear voice; and, seeing the furious scorn in her face, Reddin silently turned away.

Laurette's scorn was sharpened by a sense of the bitterest disappointment. She had allowed herself to give her heart to a coward, whom she had fancied a hero. As she turned to her father, big tears forced themselves into her eyes. But the episode had passed quickly; and her distress was not observed, as all attention now turned to Goodine and his perilous undertaking. Only McElvey, who had suspected the girl's sentiments for some time, said in an undertone, "Jim Reddin ain't no coward, and don't you forget it, sis. But it *is* queer the way he'll just take anything at all from Bill

Goodine. It's somethin' we don't none of us understand."

"I reckon he does well to be scared of him," said Laurette, with her head very high in the air.

By this time Goodine had formed his plans, and had got to work. At first he called in the assistance of two other axemen, to cut certain of the piles which had no great strain upon them. This done, the assistants returned to safe quarters; and then Bill warily reviewed the situation. "He knows what he's about," murmured McElvey, with approbation, as Bill attacked another pile, cut it two-thirds through, and left it so. Then he severed completely a huge timber far on the left front of the landing. There remained but two piles to withstand the main push of the logs. One of these was in the centre, the other a little to the right, — on which side the chopper had to make his escape when the logs

At the Rough-and-Tumble Landing

began to go. This latter pile Goodine now cut half-way through. Feeling himself the hero of the hour, he handled his axe brilliantly, and soon forgot his indignation against Laurette. At length he attacked the centre pile, the key to the whole structure.

Everybody, at this point, held his breath. Loud sounded the measured axe-strokes over the rush of the swollen river. No one moved but Reddin, and no one but Laurette noticed his movement. His skilled eye had detected a danger which none of the rest perceived. He drew close to the brow, and moved a little way down the bank.

"What can he be up to?" wondered Laurette; and then she sniffed angrily because she had thought about him at all.

Goodine dealt a few cautious strokes upon the central pile, paused a moment or two to reconnoitre, and then renewed his attack. Reddin became very fidgety. He watched the logs, and shouted earnestly, —

"Better come out o' that right now and finish on this 'ere nigh pile."

Goodine looked up, eyed first his adviser, then very narrowly the logs, and answered, tersely, "Go to h—ll!"

"That's just like the both of 'em," muttered McElvey, as Goodine turned and resumed his chopping.

At this moment there came a sullen, tearing sound; and the top of the near pile, which had been half cut through, began to lean slowly, slowly. A yell of desperate warning arose. Goodine dropped his axe, turned like lightning, and made a tremendous leap for safety. He gained the edge of the landing-front, slipped on an oozy stone, and fell back with a cry of horror right beneath the toppling mass of logs.

At the Rough-and-Tumble Landing

As his cry re-echoed from every throat, Jim Reddin dropped beside him as swiftly and almost miraculously as a sparrow-hawk flashes upon its prey. With a terrific surge he swung Goodine backward and outward into the raging current, but away from the face of the impending avalanche. Then, as the logs all went with a gathering roar, he himself sprang outward in a superb leap, splashed mightily into the stream, disappeared, and came up some yards below. Side by side the two men struck out sturdily for shore, and in a couple of minutes their comrades' eager hands were dragging them up the bank.

"Did n't I *tell* you Jim Reddin was n't no coward?" said McElvey, with glistening eyes, to Laurette; and Laurette, having no other way to relieve her excitement and give vent to her revulsion of feelings, sat down on a sled and cried most illogically.

As the two dripping men approached the camp, she looked up to see a reconciliation. Presently Goodine emerged from a little knot of his companions, approached Reddin, and held out his hand.

At the Rough-and-Tumble Landing

"I ask yer pardon," said he. "You're a man, an' no mistake. It is my life I owe to you; an' I'm proud to owe it to sech as you!"

But Reddin took no notice of the outstretched hand. The direct and primitive movements of the backwoodsman's mind may seem to the sophisticated intelligence peculiar; but they are easy to comprehend. Jim Reddin quite overlooked the opportunity now offered for a display of exalted sentiment. In a harsh, deliberate voice he said,—

"An' now, Bill Goodine, you've got to stand up to me, an' we'll see which is the better man, you or me. Ever sence you growed up to be a man you've used me just as mean

At the Rough-and-Tumble Landing as you knowed how; an' now we'll fight it out right here."

At this went up a chorus of disapproval; and Goodine said, "I'll be d—d if I'm a-goin' to strike the man what's jest saved my life!"

"You needn't let *that* worry you, Bill," replied Reddin. "We're quits there. I reckon you forget as how your mother, God bless her, saved my life, some twenty year back, when you was jest a-toddlin'. An' I vowed to her I'd be good to you the very best I knowed how. An' I've kep' my vow. But now I reckon I'm quit of it; an' if you ain't a-goin' to give me satisfaction now my hands is free, then you ain't no man at all, an' I'll try an' find some way to *make* you fight!"

"Jim's right! — You've got to fight, Bill! — That's fair!" and many more exclamations of like character, showed the drift of popular sentiment so plainly that Goodine exclaimed, "Well, if you sez so, it's got to be! But I don't want to hurt you, Jim Reddin; an' lick you I kin, every day in the week, an' you know it!"

At the Rough-and-Tumble Landing

"You're a liar!" remarked Jim Reddin, in a business-like voice, as the hands formed a ring.

At this some of the hands laughed, and Goodine, glancing around, caught the ghost of a smile on Laurette's face. This was all that was needed. The blood boiled up to his temples, and with an oath under his breath he sprang upon his adversary.

Smoothly and instantaneously as a shadow Reddin eluded the attack. And now his face lost its set look of injury and assumed a smile of cheerful interest. Bill Goodine, in spite of his huge bulk, had the elasticity and dash of a panther; but his quickness was nothing to that of Reddin. Once or twice the latter parried, with seeming ease, his most destructive

At the Rough-and-Tumble Landing

lunges, but more often he contented himself with moving aside like a flash of light. Presently Goodine cried out, —

"Why don't yer *fight*, like a man, stidder skippin' out o' the road like a flea?"

"'Cause I don't want to hurt you," laughed Reddin.

But that little boastful laugh delayed his movements, and Goodine was upon him. Two or three terrible short-arm blows were exchanged, and then the two men grappled.

"Let 'em be," ordered McElvey. "They'd better wrastle than fight."

For a second or two, nay, for perhaps a whole minute, it looked to the spectators as if Reddin must be crushed helpless in Bill's tremendous embrace. Then it began to dawn on them that Reddin had captured the more deadly hold. Then the dim rumors of Reddin's marvellous strength began to gather credence, as it was seen how his grip seemed to dominate that of his great opponent.

For several minutes the straining antagonists swayed about the ring. Then suddenly Reddin straightened himself, and Bill's hold slipped for an instant. Before he could recover it Reddin had stooped, secured a lower grip, and in a moment hurled his adversary clear over his shoulder. A roar of applause went up from the spectators; and Goodine, after trying to rise, lay still and groaned, "I'm licked, Jim. I've had enough."

The boss soon pronounced that Bill's shoulder was dislocated, and that he'd have to go back to the settlements to be doctored. This being the case, Laurette said to him benevolently, after her horse was harnessed to the pung, "I'm sorry I can't ask you to drive me home, though you *did* cut out the logs, Bill. But I reckon it'll be the next best thing fur you if *I* drive *you* home. An'

At the Rough-and-Tumble Landing

Jim Reddin 'll come along, maybe, to kind of look after the both of us."

To which proposition poor Bill grinned a rather ghastly assent.

In the Accident Ward.

The grass was gray, of a strange and dreadful pallor, but long and soft. Unbroken, and bending all one way, as if to look at something, it covered the wide, low, rounded hill that rose before me. Over the hill the sky hung close, gray and thick, with the color of a parched interminable twilight. Dew or a drop of rain could not be thought of as coming from such a sky.

Along the base of the low hill ran a red road of baked clay, blood red, and beaten with nameless and innumerable feet. I stood in the middle of this road and prepared to ascend the hill obliquely by a narrow

In the Accident Ward footpath, red as blood, which divided the soft gray bending of the grasses. Behind me the road made a sharp turn, descending out of thick clouds into a little blood-red hollow, where it was crossed by an open gate. In this gate, through which I had somehow come, stood two gray leopards and a small ape. The beasts stood on tip-toe and eyed me with a dreadful curiosity; and from somewhere in the little hollow I heard a word whispered which I could not understand. But the beasts heard it, and drew away through the open gate, and disappeared.

Between the footpath (which all the time gleamed redly through the over-gathering grasses) and the rounded brink of the gulf there seemed to be a fence of some sort, so fine that I could not quite distinguish it, but which I knew to be there.

I turned my eyes to the low summit of the hill. There I saw a figure, *In the* all gray, cleaving the grasses in flight *Accident* as swift as an arrow. Behind, in *Ward* pursuit, came another figure, of the color of the grasses, tall and terrible beyond thought. This being, as it seemed to me, was the Second Death, and my knees trembled with horror and a sort of loathing. Then I saw that he who fled made directly for me; and as they sped I could hear a strange hissing and rustling of their garments cleaving the grasses. When the fleeing ghost reached me, and fell at my feet, and clasped my knees in awful fear, I felt myself grow strong, and all dread left my soul. I reached forth my right hand and grasped the pursuing horror by the throat.

I heard the being laugh, and the iron grip of my own strong and implacable fingers seemed to close with a keen agony upon my own throat, and a curtain seemed to fall over my

In the Accident Ward eyes. Then I gasped for breath, and a warm pungent smell clung in my nostrils, and a white light swam into my eyes, and I heard a voice murmuring far off, but in an accent strangely familiar and commonplace, "He's coming round all right now."

I opened my eyes with a dim wonder, and found myself surrounded by the interested faces of the doctors and the clean white walls of the hospital ward. I heard a sound of some one breathing hoarsely near by, and a white-capped nurse with kind eyes stepped up to my pillow, and I perceived that the heavy breather was myself. I was lying with my head and neck swathed in bandages, and a sharp pain at my throat. Then flashed across my memory the crash and sickening upheaval of the collision. I wondered feebly how it had fared with my fellow-passengers, and again I saw that instant's vision of wild and startled faces as the crowded car rose and pitched downward, I knew not whither. With a sense of inexpressible weariness, my brain at once allowed the terrible scene to slip from its grasp, and I heard a doctor, who was standing at the bedside watch in hand, say, quietly, "He'll sleep now for a couple of hours."

The Perdu.

To the passing stranger there was nothing mysterious about it except the eternal mystery of beauty. To the scattered folk, however, who lived their even lives within its neighborhood, it was an object of dim significance and dread.

At first sight it seemed to be but a narrow, tideless, windless bit of backwater; and the first impulse of the passing stranger was to ask how it came to be called the " Perdu." On this point he would get little information from the folk of the neighborhood, who knew not French. But if he were to translate the term for their better information, they would show themselves impressed by a sense of its occult appropriateness.

The whole neighborhood was one wherein the strange and the not-to-be-understood might feel at home. It was a place where the unusual was not felt to be impossible. Its peace was the peace of one entranced. To its expectancy a god might come, or a monster, or nothing more than the realization of eventless weariness.

Only four or five miles away, across the silent, bright meadows and beyond a softly swelling range of pastured hills, swept the great river, a busy artery of trade.

On the river were all the modern noises, and with its current flowed the stream of modern ideas. Within sight of the river a mystery, or anything uninvestigated, or aught unamenable to the spirit of the age, would have seemed an anachronism. But back here, among the tall wildparsnip tops and the never-stirring

The Perdu clumps of orange lilies, life was different, and dreams seemed likely to come true.

The Perdu lay perpetually asleep, along beside a steep bank clothed with white birches and balsam poplars. Amid the trunks of the trees grew elder shrubs, and snake-berries, and the elvish trifoliate plants of the purple and the painted trillium. The steep bank, and the grove, and the Perdu with them, ran along together for perhaps a quarter of a mile, and then faded out of existence, absorbed into the bosom of the meadows.

The Perdu was but a stone's throw broad, throughout its entire length. The steep with its trunks and leafage formed the northern bound of it; while its southern shore was the green verge of the meadows. Along this low rim its whitish opalescent waters mixed smoothly with the roots and over-hanging blades of

the long grasses, with the cloistral
arched frondage of the ferns, and
with here and there a strayed spray
of purple wild-pea. Here and there,
too, a clump of Indian willow
streaked the green with the vivid
crimson of its stems.

Everything watched and waited.
The meadow was a sea of sun mysteriously imprisoned in the green
meshes of the grass-tops. At wide
intervals arose some lonely alder
bushes, thick banked with clematis.
Far off, on the slope of a low, bordering hill, the red doors of a barn
glowed ruby-like in the transfiguring
sun. At times, though seldom, a
blue heron winged over the level.
At times a huge black-and-yellow bee
hummed past, leaving a trail of faint
sound that seemed to linger like a
perfume. At times the landscape,
that was so changeless, would seem
to waver a little, to shift confusedly
like things seen through running

The Perdu water. And all the while the meadow scents and the many-colored butterflies rose straight up on the moveless air, and brooded or dropped back into their dwellings.

Yet in all this stillness there was no invitation to sleep. It was a stillness rather that summoned the senses to keep watch, half apprehensively, at the doorways of perception. The wide eye noted everything, and considered it, — even to the hairy red fly alit on the fern frond, or the skirring progress of the black water-beetle across the pale surface of the Perdu. The ear was very attentive — even to the fluttering down of the blighted leaf, or the thin squeak of the bee in the straitened calyx, or the faint impish conferrings of the moisture exuding suddenly from somewhere under the bank. If a common sound, like the shriek of a steamboat's whistle, now and again soared over across the hills and fields, it was changed in that refracting atmosphere, and became a defiance at the gates of waking dream.

The lives, thoughts, manners, even the open, credulous eyes of the quiet folk dwelling about the Perdu, wore in greater or less degree the complexion of the neighborhood. How this came to be is one of those nice questions for which we need hardly expect definitive settlement. Whether the people, in the course of generations, had gradually keyed themselves to the dominant note of their surroundings, or whether the neighborhood had been little by little wrought up to its pitch of supersensibility by the continuous impact of superstitions, and expectations, and apprehensions, and wonders, and visions, rained upon it from the personalities of an imaginative and secluded people, — this might be discussed with more argument than conclusiveness.

The Perdu Of the dwellers about the Perdu none was more saturated with the magic of the place than Reuben Waugh, a boy of thirteen. Reuben lived in a small, yellow-ochre-colored cottage, on the hill behind the barn with the red doors. Whenever Reuben descended to the level, and turned to look back at the yellow dot of a house set in the vast expanse of pale blue sky, he associated the picture with a vague but haunting conception of some infinite forget-me-not flower. The boy had all the chores to do about the little homestead; but even then there was always time to dream. Besides, it was not a pushing neighborhood; and whenever he would he took for himself a half-holiday. At such times he was more than likely to stray over to the banks of the Perdu.

It would have been hard for Reuben to say just why he found the Perdu so attractive. He might have said it was the fishing; for sometimes, though not often, he would cast a timorous hook into its depths and tremble lest he should lure from the pallid waters some portentous and dreadful prey. He never captured, however, anything more terrifying than catfish; but these were clad in no small measure of mystery, for the white waters of the Perdu had bleached their scales to a ghastly pallor, and the opalescence of their eyes was apt to haunt their captor's reveries. He might have said, also, that it was his playmate, little Celia Hansen, — whose hook he would bait whenever she wished to fish, and whose careless hands, stained with berries, he would fill persistently with bunches of the hot-hued orange lily.

But Reuben knew there was more to say than this. In a boyish way, and all unrealizing, he loved the child with a sort of love that would

The Perdu one day flower out as an absorbing passion. For the present, however, important as she was to him, she was nevertheless distinctly secondary to the Perdu itself with its nameless spell. If Celia was not there, and if he did not care to fish, the boy still longed for the Perdu, and was more than content to lie and watch for he knew not what, amid the rapt herbage, and the brooding insects, and the gnome-like conspiracies of the moisture exuding far under the bank.

Celia was two years younger than Reuben, and by nature somewhat less imaginative. For a long time she loved the Perdu primarily for its associations with the boy who was her playmate, her protector, and her hero. When she was about seven years old Reuben had rescued her from an angry turkey-cock, and had displayed a confident firmness which seemed to her wonderfully fine. Hence had arisen an unformulated but enduring faith that Reuben could be depended upon in any emergency. From that day forward she had refused to be content with other playmates. Against this uncompromising preference Mrs. Hansen was wont to protest rather plaintively; for there were social grades even here, and Mrs. Hansen, whose husband's acres were broad (including the Perdu itself), knew well that "that Waugh boy" was not her Celia's equal.

The profound distinction, however, was not one which the children could appreciate; and on Mrs. Hansen lay the spell of the neighborhood, impelling her to wait for whatever might see fit to come to pass.

For these two children the years that slipped so smoothly over the Perdu were full of interest. They met often. In the spring, when the

The Perdu Perdu was sullen and unresponsive, and when the soggy meadows showed but a tinge of green through the brown ruin of the winter's frosts, there was yet the grove to visit. Here Reuben would make deep incisions in the bark of the white birches, and gather tiny cupfuls of the faint-flavored sap, which, to the children's palates, had all the relish of nectar. A little later on there were the blossoms of the trillium to be plucked, — blossoms whose beauty was the more alluring in that they were supposed to be poisonous.

But it was with the deepening of the summer that the spell of the Perdu deepened to its most enthralling potency. And as the little girl grew in years and came more and more under her playmate's influence, her imagination deepened as the summer deepens, her perception quickened and grew subtle. Then in a quiet fashion, a strange thing came about. Under the influence of the children's sympathetic expectancy, the Perdu began to find fuller expression. Every mysterious element in the neighborhood — whether emanating from the Perdu itself or from the spirits of the people about it — appeared to find a focus in the personalities of the two children. All the weird, formless stories, — rather suggestions or impressions than stories, — that in the course of time had gathered about the place, were revived with added vividness and awe. New ones, too, sprang into existence all over the country-side, and were certain to be connected, soon after their origin, with the name of Reuben Waugh. To be sure, when all was said and sifted, there remained little that one could grasp or set down in black and white for question. Every experience, every manifestation, when investigated, seemed to resolve itself into something of an epidemic

The Perdu sense of unseen but thrilling influences.

The only effect of all this, however, was to invest Reuben with an interest and importance that consorted curiously with his youth. With a certain consciousness of superiority, born of his taste for out-of-the-way reading, and dreaming, and introspection, the boy accepted the subtle tribute easily, and was little affected by it. He had the rare fortune not to differ in essentials from his neighbors, but only to intensify and give visible expression to the characteristics latent in them all.

Thus year followed year noiselessly, till Reuben was seventeen and Celia fifteen. For all the expectancy, the sense of eventfulness even, of these years, little had really happened save the common inexplicable happenings of life and growth. The little that might be counted an exception may be told in a few words.

The customs of angling for catfish *The* and tapping the birch trees for sap, *Perdu* had been suffered to fall into disuse. Rather, it seemed interesting to wander vaguely together, or in the long grass to read together from the books which Reuben would borrow from the cobwebby library of the old schoolmaster.

As the girl reached up mentally, or perhaps, rather, emotionally, toward the imaginative stature of her companion, her hold upon him strengthened. Of old, his perceptions had been keenest when alone, but now they were in every way quickened by her presence. And now it happened that the great blue heron came more frequently to visit the Perdu. While the children were sitting amid the birches, they heard the *hush! hush!* of the bird's wings fanning the pallid water. The bird, did I say? But it seemed to them a spirit in the guise of a bird. It

The had gradually forgotten its seclusive-
Perdu ness, and now dropped its long legs at a point right over the middle of the Perdu, alighted apparently on the liquid surface, and stood suddenly transformed into a moveless statue of a bird, gazing upon the playmates with bright, significant eyes. The look made Celia tremble.

The Perdu, as might have been expected when so many mysteries were credited to it, was commonly held to be bottomless. It is a very poor neighborhood indeed, that cannot show a pool with this distinction. Reuben, of course, knew the interpretation of the myth. He knew the Perdu was very deep. Except at either end, or close to the banks, no bottom could be found with such fathom-lines as he could command. To him, and hence to Celia, this idea of vast depths was thrillingly suggestive, and yet entirely believable. The palpably impossible had small

"A MOVELESS STATUE OF A BIRD."

appeal for them. But when first they saw the great blue bird alight where they knew the water was fathoms deep, they came near being surprised. At least, they felt the pleasurable sensation of wonder. How was the heron supported on the water? From their green nest the children gazed and gazed; and the great blue bird held them with the gem-like radiance of its unwinking eye. At length to Reuben came a vision of the top of an ancient treetrunk just beneath the bird's feet, just beneath the water's surface. Down, slanting far down through the opaline opaqueness, he saw the huge trunk extend itself, to an immemorial root-hold in the clayey, perpendicular walls of the Perdu. He unfolded the vision to Celia, who understood. "And it's just as wonderful," said the girl, "for how did the trunk get there?"

"That's so," answered Reuben,

with his eyes fixed on the bird, — "but then it's quite possible!"

And at the low sound of their voices the bird winnowed softly away.

At another time, when the children were dreaming by the Perdu, a far-off dinner-horn sounded, hoarsely but sweetly, its summons to the workers in the fields. It was the voice of noon. As the children, rising to go, glanced together across the Perdu, they clasped each other with a start of mild surprise. "Did you see that?" whispered Celia.

"What did you see?" asked the boy.

"It looked like a pale green hand, that waved for a moment over the water, and then sank," said Celia.

"Yes," said Reuben, "that's just what it looked like. But I don't believe it really was a hand! You see those thin lily-leaves all about the spot? Their stems are long, wonderfully long and slender. If one of those queer, whitish catfish, like we used to catch, were to take hold of a lily-stem and pull hard, the edges of the leaf might rise up and wave just the way *that* did! You can't tell what the catfish won't do down there!"

"Perhaps that's all it was," said Celia.

"Though we can't be sure," added Reuben.

And thereafter, whensoever that green hand seemed to wave to them across the pale water, they were content to leave the vision but half explained.

It also came to pass, as unexpectedly as anything could come to pass by the banks of the Perdu, that one dusky evening, as the boy and girl came slowly over the meadows, they saw a radiant point of light that wavered fitfully above the water. They watched it in silence. As it came to

<small>*The Perdu*</small> a pause, the girl said in her quiet voice, —

"It has stopped right over the place where the heron stands!"

"Yes," replied Reuben, "it is evidently a will-o'-the-wisp. The queer gas, which makes it, comes perhaps from the end of that dead tree-trunk, just under the surface."

But the fact that the point of light was thus explicable, made it no less interesting and little less mysterious to the dwellers about the Perdu. As it came to be an almost nightly feature of the place, the people supplemented its local habitation with a name, calling it "Reube Waugh's Lantern." Celia's father, treating the Perdu and all that pertained to it with a reverent familiarity befitting his right of proprietorship, was wont to say to Reuben, —

"Who gave you leave, Reuben, to hoist your lantern on my property? If you don't take it away pretty soon, I'll be having the thing put in pound."

It may be permitted me to cite yet one more incident to illustrate more completely the kind of events which seemed of grave importance in the neighborhood of the Perdu. It was an accepted belief that, even in the severest frosts, the Perdu could not be securely frozen over. Winter after winter, to be sure, it lay concealed beneath such a covering of snow as only firm ice could be expected to support. Yet this fact was not admitted in evidence. Folks said the ice and snow were but a film, waiting to yield upon the slightest pressure. Furthermore, it was held that neither bird nor beast was ever known to tread the deceptive expanse. No squirrel track, no slim, sharp foot-mark of partridge, traversed the immaculate level. One winter, after a light snowfall in the night, as Reuben strayed into the

The Perdu low-ceilinged kitchen of the Hansen farm-house, Mr. Hansen remarked in his quaint, dreamy drawl, —

"What for have you been walking on the Perdu, Reuben? This morning, on the new snow, I saw foot-marks of a human running right across it. It must have been you, Reuben. There's nobody else round here 'd do it!"

"No," said Reuben, "I have n't been nigh the Perdu these three days past. And then I did n't try walking on it, any way."

"Well," continued Celia's father, "I suppose folks would call it queer! Those foot-marks just began at one side of the Perdu, and ended right up sharp at the other. There was n't another sign of a foot, on the meadow or in the grove!"

"Yes," assented Reuben, "it looks queer in a way. But then, it 's easy for the snow to drift over the other tracks; while the Perdu lies low out of the wind." *The Perdu*

The latter days of Reuben's stay beside the banks of the Perdu were filled up by a few events like these, by the dreams which these evoked, and above all by the growing realization of his love for Celia. At length the boy and girl slipped unawares into mutual self-revelations; and for a day or two life seemed so materially and tangibly joyous that vision and dream eluded them. Then came the girl's naïve account of how her confidences had been received at home. She told of her mother's objections, soon overruled by her father's obstinate plea that "Reuben Waugh, when he got to be a man grown, would be good enough for any girl alive."

Celia had dwelt with pride on her father's championship of their cause. Her mother's opposition she had been familiar with for as long as

The Perdu she could remember. But it was the mother's opposition that loomed large in Reuben's eyes.

First it startled him with a vague sense of disquiet. Then it filled his soul with humiliation as its full significance grew upon him. Then he formed a sudden resolve; and neither the mother's relenting cordiality, nor the father's practical persuasions, nor Celia's tears, could turn him from his purpose. He said that he would go away, after the time-honored fashion, and seek his fortune in the world. He vowed that in three or four years, when they would be of a fit age to marry, he would come back with a full purse and claim Celia on even terms. This did not suit the unworldly old farmer, who had inherited, not in vain, the spiritualities and finer influences of his possession, the Perdu. He desired, first of all, his girl's happiness. He rebuked Reuben's pride with a sternness unusual for *The Perdu* him. But Reuben went.

He went down the great river. Not many miles from the quiet region of the Perdu there was a little riverside landing, where Reuben took the steamer and passed at once into another atmosphere, another world. The change was a spiritual shock to him, making him gasp as if he had fallen into a tumultuous sea. There was the same chill, there was a like difficulty in getting his balance. But this was not for long. His innate self-reliance steadied him rapidly. His long-established habit of superiority helped him to avoid betraying his first sense of ignorance and unfitness. His receptiveness led him to assimilate swiftly the innumerable and novel facts of life with which he came all at once in contact; and he soon realized that the stirring, capable crowd, whose ready handling of affairs had at first

The Perdu overawed him, was really inferior in true insight to the peculiar people whom he had left about the Perdu. He found that presently he himself could handle the facts of life with the light dexterity which had so amazed him; but through it all he preserved (as he could see that those about him did not) his sense of the relativity of things. He perceived, always, the dependence of the facts of life upon the ideas underlying them, and thrusting them forward as manifestations or utterances. With his undissipated energy, his curious frugality in the matter of self-revelation, and his instinctive knowledge of men, he made his way from the first, and the roaring port at the mouth of the great river yielded him of its treasures for the asking. This was in a quiet enough way, indeed, but a way that more than fulfilled his expectations; and in the height of the blossoming time of his fifth summer in the world he found him-self rich enough to go back to the Perdu and claim Celia. He resolved that he would buy property near the Perdu and settle there. He had no wish to live in the world; but to the world he would return often, for the sake of the beneficence of its friction, — as a needle, he thought, is the keener for being thrust often amid the grinding particles of the emery-bag. He resigned his situation and went aboard an up-river boat, — a small boat that would stop at every petty landing, if only to put ashore an old woman or a bag of meal, if only to take in a barrel of potatoes or an Indian with baskets and bead-work.

About mid-morning of the second day, at a landing not a score of miles below the one whereat Reuben would disembark, an Indian did come aboard with baskets and bead-work. At sight of him the old atmosphere

The Perdu of expectant mystery came over Reuben as subtly as comes the desire of sleep. He had seen this same Indian — he recognized the unchanging face — on the banks of the Perdu one morning years before, brooding motionless over the motionless water. Reuben began unconsciously to divest himself of his lately gathered worldliness; his mouth softened, his eyes grew wider and more passive, his figure fell into looser and freer lines, his dress seemed to forget its civil trimness. When at length he had disembarked at the old wharf under the willows, had struck across through the hilly sheep-pastures, and had reached a slope overlooking the amber-bright country of the Perdu, he was once more the silently eager boy, the quaintly reasoning visionary, his spirit waiting alert at his eyes and at his ears.

Reuben had little concern for the

highways. Therefore he struck *The* straight across the meadows, through *Perdu* the pale green vetch-tangle, between the intense orange lilies, amid the wavering blue butterflies and the warm, indolent perfumes of the wild-parsnip. As he drew near the Perdu there appeared the giant blue heron, dropping to his perch in mid-water. In almost breathless expectancy Reuben stepped past a clump of red willows, banked thick with clematis. His heart was beating quickly, and he could hear the whisper of the blood in his veins, as he came once more in view of the still, white water.

His gaze swept the expanse once and again, then paused, arrested by the unwavering, significant eye of the blue heron. The next moment he was vaguely conscious of a hand, that seemed to wave once above the water, far over among the lilies. He smiled as he said to him-

The Perdu self that nothing had changed. But at this moment the blue heron, as if disturbed, rose and winnowed reluctantly away; and Reuben's eyes, thus liberated, turned at once to the spot where he had felt, rather than seen, the vision. As he looked the vision came again,—a hand, and part of an arm, thrown out sharply as if striving to grasp support, then dropping back and bearing down the lily leaves. For an instant Reuben's form seemed to shrink and cower with horror,— and the next he was cleaving with mighty strokes the startled surface of the Perdu. That hand—it was not pale green, like the waving hand of the old, childish vision. It was white and the arm was white, and white the drenched lawn sleeve clinging to it. He had recognized it, he knew not how, for Celia's.

Reaching the edge of the lily patch, Reuben dived again and

again, groping desperately among the long, serpent-like stems. The Perdu at this point — and even in his horror he noted it with surprise — was comparatively shallow. He easily got the bottom and searched it minutely. The edge of the dark abyss, into which he strove in vain to penetrate, was many feet distant from the spot where the vision had appeared. Suddenly, as he rested, breathless and trembling, on the grassy brink of the Perdu, he realized that this, too, was but a vision. It was but one of the old mysteries of the Perdu; and it had taken for him that poignant form, because his heart and brain were so full of Celia. With a sigh of exquisite relief he thought how amused she would be at his plight, but how tender when she learned the cause of it. He laughed softly; and just then the blue heron came back to the Perdu.

The Perdu Reuben shook himself, pressed some of the water from his dripping clothes, and climbed the steep upper bank of the Perdu. As he reached the top he paused among the birch trees to look back upon the water. How like a floor of opal it lay in the sun; then his heart leaped into his throat suffocatingly, for again rose the hand and arm, and waved, and dropped back among the lilies! He grasped the nearest tree, that he might not, in spite of himself, plunge back into the pale mystery of the Perdu. He rubbed his eyes sharply, drew a few long breaths to steady his heart, turned his back doggedly on the shining terror, and set forward swiftly for the farmhouse, now in full view not three hundred yards away.

For all the windless, down-streaming summer sunshine, there was that in Reuben's drenched clothes which chilled him to the heart. As he reached the wide-eaved cluster of the farmstead, a horn in the distance blew musically for noon. It was answered by another and another. But no such summons came from the kitchen door to which his feet now turned. The quiet of the Seventh Day seemed to possess the wide, bright farm-yard. A flock of white ducks lay drowsing on a grassy spot. A few hens dusted themselves with silent diligence in the ash-heap in front of the shed; and they stopped to watch with bright eyes the stranger's approach. From under the apple-trees the horses whinnied to him lonesomely. It was very peaceful; but the peacefulness of it bore down upon Reuben's soul like lead. It seemed as if the end of things had come. He feared to lift the latch of the well-known door.

As he hesitated, trembling, he observed that the white blinds were

The Perdu down at the sitting-room windows. The window nearest him was open, and the blind stirred almost imperceptibly. Behind it, now, his intent ear caught a sound of weary sobbing. At once he seemed to see all that was in the shadowed room. The moveless, shrouded figure, the unresponding lips, the bowed heads of the mourners, all came before him as clearly as if he were standing in their midst. He leaned against the door-post, and at this moment the door opened. Celia's father stood before him.

The old man's face was drawn with his grief. Something of bitterness came into his eyes as he looked on Reuben.

"You've heard, then!" he said harshly.

"I know!" shaped itself inaudibly on Reuben's lips.

At the sight of his anguish the old man's bitterness broke.

"You've come in time for the funeral," he exclaimed piteously. "Oh, Reube, if you'd stayed it might have been different!"

The Romance of an Ox-Team.

The oxen, lean and rough-haired, one of them carroty red, the other brindle and white, were slouching inertly along the narrow backwoods road. From habit they sagged heavily on the yoke, and groaned huge windy sighs, although the vehicle they were hauling held no load. This structure, the mere skeleton of a cart, consisted of two pairs of clumsy, broad-tired wheels, united by a long tongue of ash, whose tip was tied with rope to the middle of the forward axle. The road looked innocent of even the least of the country-road-master's well-meaning attempts at repair, — a circumstance,

"SLOUCHING INERTLY ALONG THE NARROW BACKWOODS ROAD."

indeed, which should perhaps be set to its credit. It was made up of four deep, parallel ruts, the two outermost eroded by years of journeying cart-wheels, the inner ones worn by the companioning hoofs of many a yoke of oxen. Down the centre ran a high and grassy ridge, intolerable to the country parson and the country doctor, compelled to traverse this highway in their one-horse wagons. From ruts and ridges alike protruded the imperishable granite boulder, which wheels and feet might polish but never efface. On either side of the roadway was traced an erratic furrow, professing to do duty for a drain, and at intervals emptying a playful current across the track to wander down the ruts.

Along beside the slouching team slouched a tall, lank, stoop-shouldered youth, the white down just beginning to stiffen into bristles on his long upper lip. His pale eyes and pale hair looked yet paler by contrast with his thin, red, wind-roughened face. In his hand he carried a long-handled ox-whip, with a short goad in the butt of it.

"Gee, Buck!" he drawled, prodding the near ox lightly in the ribs. And the team lurched to the right to avoid a markedly obtrusive boulder. "Haw, Bright!" he ejaculated a minute later, flicking with his whip the off shoulder of the farther ox. And with sprawling legs and swaying of hind-quarters the team swerved obediently to the left, shunning a mire-hole that would have taken in the wheel to the hub. Presently, coming to a swampy spot that stretched all the way across the road, the youth seated himself sidewise on the narrow tongue connecting the fore and hind axles, and drove his team dry-shod.

It was a slow and creaking progress; but there seemed to be no hurry, and the youth dreamed gloomily on his jolting perch. His eyes took no note of the dark-mossed, scrubby hillocks, the rough clearings blackened with fire, the confused and ragged woods, as they crept past in sombre procession. But suddenly, as the cart rounded a turn in the road, there came into view the figure of a girl travelling in the same direction. The young man slipped from his perch and prodded up the oxen to a brisk walk.

The Romance of an Ox-Team

As the noise of the team approached her, the girl looked around. She was good to see, with her straight, vigorous young figure in its blue-gray homespun gown. Her hair, in color not far from that of the red ox, was rich and abundant, and lay in a coil so gracious that not even the tawdry millinery of her cheap "store" hat could make her head look quite commonplace. Her face was freckled, but wholesome and comely. A shade of displeasure passed over it as she saw who was behind her, and she hastened her steps perceptibly. But presently she remembered that she had a good five miles to go ere she would reach her destination; and she realized that she could not hope to escape by flight. With a pout of vexation she resigned herself to the inevitable, and dropped back into her former pace. Immediately the ox-team overtook her.

As the oxen slowed up she stepped to the right to let them pass, and then walked on, thus placing the cart between herself and her undesired companion. The youth looked disconcerted by these tactics, and for a few moments could find nothing to say. Then, dropping his long white lashes sheepishly, he murmured, "Good-day, Liz."

"Well, Jim-Ed!" replied the girl, coolly.

"Won't ye set on an' let me give

ye a lift home?" he asked, with entreaty in his voice.

"No," she said, with finality: "I'd ruther walk."

Not knowing how to answer this rebuff, he tried to cover his embarrassment by exclaiming authoritatively, "Haw, Bright!" whereupon the team slewed to the left and crowded him into the ditch.

Soon he began again.

"Ye *might* set on, Liz," he pleaded.

"Yes, I *might*," said she, with what she considered rather withering smartness; "but I ain't a-goin' to."

"Ye'll be tired afore ye git home," he persisted, encouraged by finding that she would talk back at him.

"James-Ed A'ki'son," she declared, with emphasis, "if ye think I'm a-goin' to be beholden to *you* fer a lift home, ye're mistaken, that's all."

After this there was silence for some time, broken only by the rattling and bumping of the cart, and once by the whir of a woodcock that volleyed across the road. Young Atkinson chewed the cud of gloomy bewilderment. At length he roused himself to another effort.

"Liz," said he, plaintively, "y' ain't been like ye used to, sence ye come back from the States."

"Ain't I?" she remarked, indifferently.

"No, Liz, ye ain't," he repeated, with a sort of pathetic emphasis, as if eager to persuade himself that she had condescended to rebut his accusation. "Y' ain't been like ye used to at all. Appears like as if ye thought us folks in the Settlement was n't good enough fer ye now."

At this the girl tossed her head crossly.

"It appears like as if ye wanted to be back in the States ag'in," he continued, in a voice of anxious interrogation.

"My lands," exclaimed the girl, "but ye 're green!"

To the young man this seemed such an irrelevant remark that he was silent for some time, striving to fathom its significance. As his head sank lower and lower, and he seemed to lose himself completely in joyless revery, the girl shot occasional glances at him out of the corners of her eyes. She had spent the preceding winter in a factory in a crude but stirring little New England town, and had come back to Nova Scotia ill content with the monotony of life in the backwoods seclusion of Wyer's Settlement. Before she went away she had been, to use the vernacular of the Settlement, "keepin' company with Jim-Ed A'ki'son;" and now, to her, the young man seemed to unite and concentrate in his person all that she had been wont to persuade herself she had outgrown. To be sure, she not seldom caught herself dropping back comfortably into the old conditions. But these symptoms stirred in her heart an uneasy resentment, akin to that which she felt whenever — as would happen at times — she could not help recognizing that Jim-Ed and his affairs were not without a passing interest in her eyes.

Now she began to grow particularly angry at him because, as she thought, "he had n't nothing to say fer himself." Sadly to his disadvantage, she compared his simplicity and honest diffidence with the bold self-assertion and easy familiarity of the young fellows with whom she had come in contact during the winter. Their impertinences had offended her grievously at the time, but, woman-like, she permitted herself to forget that now, in order to accentuate the deficiencies of the man whom she was unwilling to think well of.

"My lands!" she reiterated to herself, with accumulated scorn, "but *ain't* he green? He — why, he wouldn't know a 'lectric car from a waterin'-cart. An' *soft*, too, takin' all my sass 'thout givin' me no lip back, no more 'n if I was his mother!"

But the young man presently broke in upon these unflattering reflections. With a sigh he said slowly, as if half to himself, —

"Lands, but I used to set a powerful store by ye, Liz!"

He paused; and at that "used to" the girl opened her eyes with angry apprehension. But he went on, —

"An' I set still more store by ye now, Liz, someways. Seems like I jest couldn't live without ye. I always did feel as how ye was too good, a sight too good, fer me, an' you so smart; an' now I feel it more 'n ever, bein' 's ye 've seen so much of the world like. But, Liz, I *don't* allow as it's right an' proper fer even you to look down the way ye do on the place ye was born in an' the folks ye was brung up with."

"My!" thought the girl to herself, "he's got some spunk, after all, to git off such a speech as that, an' to rake me over the coals, too!"

But aloud she retorted, "Who's a-lookin' down on anybody, Jim-Ed A'ki'son? An', anyways, *you* ain't the whole of Wyer's Settlement, be ye?"

The justice of this retort seemed to strike the young man with great force.

"That's so," he acknowledged, gloomily. "'Course I ain't. An' I s'pose I hadn't oughter said what I did."

Then he relapsed into silence. For half a mile he slouched on without a syllable, save an occasional word of command addressed to the team. Coming to another boggy bit of road, he seated himself dejectedly on the cart, and apparently would not presume to again press unwelcome assistance upon his fellow-way-farer. Quite uncertain whether to interpret this action as excess of humility or as a severe rebuke, the girl picked her way as best she could, flushed with a sense of injury.

When the mud was passed, the young man absent-mindedly kept his seat. Beginning to boil with indignation, the girl speedily lost her confident superiority, and felt humiliated. She did not know exactly what to do. She could not continue to walk humbly beside the cart. The situation was profoundly altered by the mere fact that the young man was riding. She tried to drop behind; but the team had an infinite capacity for loitering. At last, with head high in the air, she

The Romance of an Ox-Team

darted ahead of the team, and walked as fast as she could. Although she heard no orders given by their driver, she knew at once that the oxen had quickened their pace, and that she was not leaving them behind.

Presently she found herself overtaken; whereupon, with swelling heart and face averted, she dropped again to the rear. She was drawing perilously near the verge of that feminine cataclysm, tears, when Fate stepped in to save her from such a mortification.

Fate goes about in many merry disguises. At this juncture she presented herself under the aspect of two half-tipsy commercial travellers driving a single horse in a light open trap. They were driving in from the Settlement, in haste to reach the hotel at Bolton Corners before nightfall. The youth hawed his team vigorously till the nigh wheels were on the other side of the ditch, leaving a liberal share of the road for them to pass in.

But the drummers were not satisfied with this. After a glance at the bashful face and dejected attitude of the young man on the ox-cart, they decided that they wanted the whole road. When their horse's head almost touched the horns of the off ox, they stopped.

"Get out of the way there!" cried the man who held the reins, insolently.

At any other time Jim-Ed would have resented the town man's tone and words; just now he was thinking about the way Liz had changed.

"I've gi'n ye the best half o' the road, mister," he said, deprecatingly, "'n' I can't do no better fer ye than that."

"Yes, you can, too," shouted the driver of the trap; "you can give us the whole road. It won't hurt your old cart to go out in the stumps, but *we* ain't going to drive in the ditch, not by a jugful. Get over, I tell you, and be quick about it."

To this the youth made no immediate reply; but he began to forget about the girl, and to feel himself growing hot. As for the girl, she had stepped to the front, resolved to "show off" and to make very manifest to the city men her scorn for her companion. Her cheeks and eyes were flaming, and the drummers were not slow to respond to the challenge which she flashed at them from under her drooped lids.

"Ah, there, my beauty!" said the driver, his attention for a moment diverted from the question of right of way. His companion, a smallish man in striped trousers and fawn-colored overcoat, sprang lightly out of the trap, with the double purpose of clearing the road and amus-

ing himself with Liz. The saucy
smile with which she met him turned
into a frown, however, as he began
brutally kicking the knees of the
oxen to make them stand over.

The patient brutes crowded into
the ditch.

"Whoa, there! Gee, Buck!
gee, Bright!" ordered the youth,
and the team lurched back into the
road. At the same time he stepped
over the cart-beam and came forward
on the off side of the team.

"Ye'd better quit that, mister!"
he exclaimed, with a threatening note
in his voice.

"Give the lout a slap in the
mouth, and make him get out of
the way," cried the man in the
trap.

But the man in the fawn-colored
overcoat was busy. Liz was much
to his taste.

"Jump in and take a ride with
us, my pretty," said he.

But Liz shrank away, regretting her provocative glances now that she saw the kind of men she had to do with.

"Come, come," coaxed the man, "don't be shy, my blooming daisy. We'll drive you right in to the Corners and set up a good time for you." And, grasping her hand, he slipped an arm about her waist and tried to kiss her lips. As she tore herself fiercely away, she heard the man in the trap laugh loud approval. She struck at her insulter with clenched hand; but she did not touch him, for just then something happened to him. The long arm of the youth went out like a cannon-ball, and the drummer sprawled in the ditch. He nimbly picked himself up and darted upon his assailant, while the man in the trap shouted to him encouragingly, —

"Give it to him pretty, Mike."

But the young countryman caught

him by the neck with long, vise-like fingers, inexorable, and, holding him thus helpless at arm's length, struck him again heavily in the ribs, and hurled him over the ditch into a blueberry thicket, where he remained in dazed discretion.

Though of a lamb-like gentleness on ordinary occasions, the young countryman was renowned throughout the Settlement for the astonishing strength that lurked in his lean frame. At this moment he was well aroused, and Liz found herself watching him with a consuming admiration. He no longer slouched, and his pale eyes, like polished steel, shot a menacing gleam. He stepped forward and took the horse by the bridle.

"Now," said he to the driver, "I've gi'n ye half the road, an' if ye can't drive by in that I'm a-going to lead ye by, 'thout no more nonsense."

The Romance of an Ox-Team

"Let go that bridle!" yelled the driver, standing up and lashing at him with the whip.

One stroke caught the young man down the side of the face, and stung. It was a rash stroke.

"Hold the horse's head, Liz," he cried; and, leaping forward, he reached into the trap for his adversary. Heeding not at all the butt end of the whip which was brought down furiously upon his head, he wrenched the driver ignominiously from his seat, spun him around, shook him as if he had been a rag baby, and hurled him violently against a rotten stump on the other side of the ditch. The stump gave way, and the drummer splashed into a bog hole.

Nothing cows a man more quickly than a shaking combined with a ducking. Without a word the drummer hauled himself out of the slop and walked sullenly forward.

His companion joined him; and Liz, leading the horse and trap carefully past the cart, delivered them up to their owners with a sarcastic smile on her lips. Then she resumed her place beside the cart, the young man flicked the oxen gently, and the team once more got slowly under way.

As the discomfited drummers climbed into their trap, the girl, in the ardor of her suddenly adopted hero-worship, could not refrain from turning around again to triumph over them. When the men were fairly seated, and the reins gathered up for prompt departure, the smaller man turned suddenly and threw a large stone, with vindictive energy and deadly aim.

"Look out!" shrieked the girl; and the young countryman turned aside just in time to escape the full force of the missile. It grazed the side of his head, however, with such

The Romance of an Ox-Team violence as to bring him to his knees, and the blood spread throbbing out of the long cut like a scarlet veil. The drummers whipped their horse to a gallop, and disappeared.

The girl first stopped the team, with a true country-side instinct; and she was at the young man's side, sobbing with anxious fear, just as he staggered blindly to his feet. Seating him on the cart, she proceeded to stanch the bleeding with the edge of her gown. Observing this, he protested, and declared that the cut was nothing. But she would not be gainsaid, and he yielded, apparently well content under her hands. Then, tearing a strip from her colored cotton petticoat, she gently bound up the wound, not artistically, perhaps, but in every way to his satisfaction.

"If ye had n't gi'n me warnin', Liz, that there stun 'd about fixed me," he remarked.

The girl smiled happily, but said nothing.

After a long pause he spoke again.

"Seems to me ye're like what ye used to, Liz," said he, "only nicer, a sight nicer; an' y' used to be powerful nice. I allow there could n't *be* another girl so nice as you, Liz. An' what ever's made ye quit lookin' down on me, so sudden like?"

"Jim-Ed," she replied, in a caressing tone, "ef y' *ain't* got no paper collar on, ner no glas' di'mon' pin, I allow ye're a *man*. An' maybe —maybe ye're the *kind* of man I *like*, Jim-Ed."

To even such genuine modesty as Jim-Ed's this was comprehensible. Shyly and happily he reached out his hand for hers. They were both seated very comfortably on the cart-beam, so he did not consider it necessary to move. Side by side, and

The Romance of an Ox-Team   hand in hand, they journeyed homeward in a glorified silence. The oxen appeared to guide themselves very fairly. The sunset flushed strangely the roadside hillocks. The night-hawks swooped in the pale zenith with the twang of smitten chords. And from a thick maple on the edge of a clearing a hermit-thrush fluted slowly over and over his cloistral ecstasy.

On the Tantramar Dyke.

THE wind blew hard across the marshes of Tantramar and across the open bay. The yellow waters of the bay were driven into long, white-crested waves, and the deep green grass of the marshes was bowed in rushing, pallid lines. From the marshes the water was fenced back by ramparts of dyke, following the curve of the shore. The dyke was clothed with a sparse, gray-green, wind-whipped herbage, and along its narrow top ran a foot-path, irregularly worn bare. Following this path went a tall young woman with a yellow-haired child at her side. The wind wrapped roughly her blu-

On the Tantramar Dyke ish-gray homespun skirt about her knees, making it hard for her to walk; and the child, a little boy perhaps two years old, kept pulling back upon her grasp from time to time, to catch at weed or grass-top, or to push the blown curls out of his eyes. The woman grasped him securely, lest the wind should buffet him off the dyke, but to his babbling and his laughter she paid no heed. Her eyes held a grave sorrow that went curiously with so young a face; and her red lips, full but firm, were compressed as if in bitter retrospection. Like the child, she wore no hat upon the rich masses of her hair, but a blue and white calico sun bonnet, crisply ironed, hung by its strings from her arm.

In the sheltered mouth of a creek some hundreds of yards behind these two figures a boat was coming to land. It came from a brig which lay at anchor under the lee of a high point, half a mile further down the shore. Two sailors pulled upon the oars. In the stern sat a young fellow with an air of authority which proclaimed him at least first mate or second. In spite of his dignity, however, there was a boyish zest in his eyes. A mop of light hair, longer than is usually affected by seamen of English speech, came down upon his red and sturdy neck, and suggested that he had been sojourning long among foreigners. But in his face was the light of a glad homecoming. Eagerly he sprang to land as the boat touched the little wharf. With a shade of irresolution, he cast a quick glance up and down the shore. Then, muttering under his breath an exclamation of surprise and delight, he climbed the dyke, and made haste in pursuit of the woman and the child.

The wind was in their ears; the wind-beaten grass was thick and soft

On the Tantramar Dyke on the dyke-top; and they did not hear his hurrying footsteps. When he was yet half a dozen paces behind them, he called out "Libby!"

Like a flash the woman turned, starting as if the sound of his voice had stung her, and her hands went up to her bosom. As her eyes rested upon him, a hot flush spread over her comely young face. Her lips quivered an instant, then set themselves in stern and bitter lines. Turning on her heel without a syllable, she resumed her way. The child, who had clutched her knee in alarm at the strange voice, she kept hold of by the hand, so that now, the dyke being narrow, there was no room for another to walk beside her.

The man scanned ardently her trim, tall figure, and the heavy red-brown coil of hair which drooped low upon her neck. His eyes danced as they fell upon the child. His hands went out as if they would snatch the little fellow to his lips, but he checked the impulse.

"Libby," he repeated, in a tone of mingled confidence and coaxing, "I've come back to make it all right to you — an' the boy! I jest *could n't* git here no sooner!"

His words fell unheeded, except that the boy half turned a smiling face, and babbled shyly at him.

"Libby," he repeated, anxiously, the confidence fading out of his voice, "won't ye speak to a feller?" and after hesitating a moment for response, he stepped forward, and grasped her arm appealingly.

She caught her breath, and he thought she was going to relent; but the next instant, dropping her hold upon the child, she swung around the other arm, and struck him fiercely across the face with her open hand.

He fell back a pace or two, and

On the Tantramar Dyke stared about him foolishly, as if he thought some one on the distant ship or in the upland village might have seen his discomfiture. He felt furtively at his smarting lips, and was on the point of laughing, but changed his mind. His brows creased themselves in anxious concern, and for a good five minutes he walked behind the woman without a word. The problem he was facing grew suddenly very serious in his eyes. He had always had a vague consciousness that Libby was in some way different from the other girls of his little fishing-village; but this perception had become obscured to him in the hour when he found that she actually returned his love and could be melted by his passion. Now, however, the feeling returned to him with new force. Being a young man, he had been wont to flatter himself that he knew the "women-folks" through and through; but now he tasted a sensation of doubt and diffidence.

On the Tantramar Dyke

At length, coming up close behind her, that the wind might not blow his words away, he began, very humbly.

"Won't ye try to fergive me, Libby?" he pleaded. "I mean square, I do, so help me God. If ye knowed how I 've been a-hungerin' fer a tech of yer hand, all this long v'yage, ye 'd maybe not think so hard o' me. I ain't never cared fer no other girl but you — never really cared. I always hev wanted jest you, an' now I want ye that powerful I can't begin to tell ye — you an' the boy — the little lad — what 's a-smiling at me now, ef his mother won't."

He paused to see if his words were producing any effect, and seeing none, he went on yet more anxiously, while the furrows deepened in his forehead.

"An' now I 'm a-goin' to do the

[187]

On the Tantramar Dyke

right thing by you an' the little lad," — here the resentment darkened in the woman's face, but he could not see it, — "an' ef ye 'll come to the minister with me this day, I lay out to never let ye repent it. Freights is low, an' I kin stay home the rest of the summer, an' I 've brought ye back a tidy little lump of money in my — "

But at mention of the money the woman faced about, and confronted him with such hot indignation that he was too bewildered to finish his sentence. She opened her mouth to speak, but only uttered a sob, and in spite of herself the tears broke from her eyes. Dashing the corner of her apron across her face, she turned and walked on more hastily than before.

The man looked discouraged, then impatient, then determined. But he continued more humbly than ever.

"I know I done wrong, I know I was a mean sneak to leave ye in the lurch the way I done that spring, Libby. But I could n't help it — kind of. Stidder comin' right back here from New York an' marryin' ye, like I 'd laid out to do, honest, I had to ship in a barquentine of Purdy's that was loadin' for Bonus Ayrs. An' then we went round up the Chili coast way up to Peru fer nitrates. An' there bein' war between Chili an' Peru, an' the Chilians offerin' good pay, I 'listed, an' saw it through, an' so — "

As an explanation this was all so awkward and glaringly insufficient that the girl was excited out of her reserve. Again she turned, and this time she spoke.

"Jim Calligan," said she, fiercely, "you are lyin' to me right along. You *could n't help* leavin' me to my shame, eh? What kind of talk 's that fer a *man*? Why don't you say right out that, havin' had all you wanted of me, you jest did n't

On the Tantramar Dyke care *what* become of me, an' you jest shipped yerself off fer Bonus Ayrs as the easiest way of gittin' quit of me? An' — an' I 'd see me an' the — the babe, both of us, starve to death afore I 'd tech a cent of your money."

She ended in a fresh burst of noiseless tears, pulled the child close to her side, and walked on.

The man braced himself, as if about to use an argument which he would fain have avoided.

"Libby," said he, "I did n't want to tell ye the hull truth, but I reckon I 've got to. Ye see, I cleared out to South Ameriky jest because, fer awhile there, I thought as how the babe — was n't agoin' to be mine."

She had turned again, and was gazing at him with a look that made him feel ashamed to lift his face; but he went on.

"As true as I 'm a-standin' here, Libby, I believed it, an' it nigh killed me, I tell you. The way it come, I could n't *help* believin' it. But three months back I found out as how I 'd been deceived, and that jest made me so glad, I never thought half enough about the wicked wrong I 'd been doin' ye all this time. I was in —"

On the Tantramar Dyke

"Who told you such a wicked, wicked lie?" interrupted the woman.

"Pete Simmons," said he, simply.

"And you let him?" she demanded, with eyes flaming.

"Not much — that is, not exactly," said the man. "It was all in a letter his sister writ him."

"What, Martha, that died last spring?" she asked, eagerly.

"The very same," said he. "And Pete did n't believe it at first, no more 'n I did. *Pete* was all right, an' advised me as how I 'd oughter write ye about it an' clear it all up. But Marthy's letter looked so straight, by and by I did n't see how to get over it. She had it all down fine, how you 'd been goin' with Jud Prescott behind my back; an' how Jud had as good as owned up to her about it, an' was powerful amused at the way you an' he was foolin' me. Marthy writ as how I was too fine a feller to be treated that way, an' she jest could n't stand it. So then—"

"Well, what then?" asked the woman, in a hard voice, as he hesitated.

"Then, fer awhile, I did n't care ef I died; an' I went away to South Ameriky."

"An' what 's brought ye back now?" she inquired, in the same hard voice.

"When Marthy was on her deathbed she writ to Pete, tellin' him she 'd lied about ye, all on account — on account of a kind of a hankerin' she had fer me," explained the man, with a self-conscious hesitation. "An', oh, Libby!" he continued, in a burst of eager passion, "my heart's *achin'* fer ye, an' I do so want the little lad, an' can't ye try an' fergive me all the wrong ye've suffered through me?"

The expression on the woman's face had undergone a change — but she did not choose to let him see her face just then. She looked across the marshes, and out on the flooding tide, and wondered what made the picture so glowingly beautiful, even like her childhood's memories of it. Her very walk became unconsciously softer and more yieldingly graceful.

But she was determined not to pardon him too quickly. Without turning her face, she declared, emphatically:

"Jim Calligan, ef ye was the only man in the world, I would n't marry ye. Don't ye dare to lay a finger on me, or I'll fling the boy an' myself both into the bito yonder."

The aboideau, or, as the fisher-folk of the neighborhood were wont to

On the Tantramar Dyke — call it, the "bito," was a place where the dyke, here become a lofty and massive embankment, crossed a small creek or tidal stream. The essential feature of an aboideau is its tide-gates, so arranged as to give egress to the fresh waters of the creek, while not admitting the great tides of the bay to drown the marshes. The gates of this aboideau, however, were out of repair, and most imperfectly performed their functions. The deep basin behind the dyke was half-filled with the pale water of the creek, through which boiled up a furious yellow torrent where the tide was forcing an entrance.

In a moment or two they were on top of the aboideau. The man was silent in something like despair, deeming his case almost hopeless at the very moment when the woman was wondering how she could most gracefully capitulate. She half-turned her face, being much moved to look at him and judge from his countenance as to whether she had punished him enough. At this instant a splendid red and black butterfly hovered close before the child's eyes, and settled on a milk-weed top, just over the edge of the dyke. The child slipped from his mother's grasp, reached eagerly out to catch the gorgeous insect, and tumbled headlong into the seething turmoil of the basin.

Uttering a faint cry of horror, the woman made as if to spring in after him. But the man grasped her roughly, thrust her back, and cried, in a voice of abrupt command, "Stop there!"

Then he plunged to the rescue.

As the little one came to the surface, the man grasped him. A few powerful strokes brought them to the shore; and he was already struggling up the slippery steep with his burden as the woman, who had scrambled down the dyke and run

On the Tantramar Dyke along the brink, paused in the bordering grass and stretched out both hands to help him.

Without a word, he put the dripping, sobbing little form into her arms. She snuggled it to her bosom, devouring the wet and frightened face with her lips. Then she handed the child back to him, saying:

"Seems to me ye know how to take care of him, Jim!"

She was smiling at him through her tears in a way he could hardly fail to understand.

"An' of you, too, Libby?" he pleaded, drawing her to him, so that he held both mother and child in the one clasp.

"May be, Jim, if ye 're *quite* sure now ye want to," she assented, yielding and leaning against him.

And the wind piped on steadily above their heads; but there in the sun, under the shelter of the dyke, the peace was undisturbed.

The Hill of Chastisement.

The cave-mouth wherein I dwelt, doing night-long penance for my sin, was midway of the steep slope of the hill. The hill, naked and rocky, rose into a darkness of gray mist. Below, it fell steeply into the abyss, which was full of the blackness of a rolling smoke. Rolling silently, the smoke sometimes came up full-bosomed and as it were in haste, brimming the gulf to within a little of my feet. Again it shrank away into the depth, leaving bare the terrific ribs of the hill, upon which I feared greatly to turn my eyes; and ever through the upward roll of the smoke flamed grinning faces, as the white faces of the drowned gleam up through a black water. Sometimes the grinning faces in the smoke laughed thinly, in a whisper; but I heard it in the stillness. They waited, expecting my rejection. Then I lashed myself the more fiercely with the knotted leather scourge that hung from my girdle, and threw myself down, with prayers and cries, at the low stone barrier which cut me off from the sanctuary of the inner cave.

In the heart of the sanctuary, far withdrawn, sat an old man, a saint, in a glory of clear and pure light, so penetrating that it revealed the secrets of my breast, yet so strictly reserved that no least beam of its whiteness escaped to pierce the dread of the outer gloom. He sat with grave head bowed continually over a book that shone like crystal, and his beard fell to his feet.

In all these days that I had dwelt in the outer cave, he never once had lifted his eyes to my prayers, but I believed that the hour would come when he should look up, and I should know that my atonement was accepted. To hasten that hour I scourged myself the more furiously till the dull blood was reluctant to flow. Then I wept and prayed, and beat my forehead on the stone barrier.

The Hill of Chastisement

On the last night, it seemed that the gray mist came further down the mountainside as I scourged myself. The smoke and the faces rolled higher from the abyss as I petitioned; and in my fear I clutched at the barrier, craving leave to enter and be safe. My eyes clung to the calm form within, in its sanctuary of light.

Then suddenly I grew aware that I must go out upon the hill, and tread a rough path which ran from the

The Hill of Chastisement

cave mouth, skirting the gulf of faces. I knew that the path led all about the hill, coming again to the cave from the other side. I knew that if, treading that path and escaping the smoke and the faces, I could come again to the cave from the other side, the holy eyes would lift and look upon me from the sanctuary of light.

I drew the hooded gown about my shoulders, girt up the skirt, knotted the scourge about my middle, and set forth, trembling. And as I set forth the gloom deepened, the thin laughter from the faces in the smoke grew more shrill.

At the first I ran with speed, though the path was difficult, being confused with a jumble of squarish stones. But my hope was quickly blotted out under a sense of nameless desolation. Far across the rolling of the smoke and faces I saw a peaceful evening country-side and secure cottages, their windows warm

"AS I SET FORTH THE GLOOM DEEPENED."

with the hearth-fire lights. Through the walls of the cottages, as if they had been glass and close at hand, my eyes pierced longingly; and I saw therein safety and love. My forsakenness overwhelmed me. Then a shadow arose out of the gulf and hid the vision; and I pushed on, nigh hopeless. My knees were weakened, and I dragged my feet with labor, often falling among the stones. Each time that I fell it seemed to me that the rolling smoke swelled higher, like a tide; the faces grew more numerous and near; the thin voices rang shriller at my heels.

The Hill of Chastisement

Again and again I fell, to rise bleeding and stumble on, till suddenly I seemed to know my atonement was refused. A voice cried aloud in my heart that I was rejected.

The last of my strength went out, and my knees were like water. Yet

The Hill of Chastisement

I would not lie yielding where I fell. By the rough edges of the rocks I dragged myself forward. I wound myself yet further along the way. By this it was dark, or else my eyes had failed me, and all the air was full of the thin laughter of the faces. But a certain grayness, a little aside from the path, revealed to me a tumbled heap of stones, with some two feet of the base of a wooden pillar rising out of it. The rest was hidden. But I knew, I knew it was a wayside calvary. I knew it was set up on the hillside for the last refuge of such lost ones as I. My heart almost broke with joy. I cried out hoarsely, threw myself upon the heap, and clung with both arms to the base of the wooden upright.

As I grasped my sanctuary, the air rang with loud laughter; the faces, coming out of the smoke, sprang wide-eyed and flaming close about me; a red flare shattered the darkness. Clutching importunately, I lifted up my eyes. My refuge was not a calvary. I saw it clear. It was a reeking gibbet.

The Hill of Chastisement

Captain Joe and Jamie.

How the wind roared in from the sea over the Tantramar dike!

It was about sunset, and a fierce orange-red gleam, thrusting itself through a rift in the clouds that blackened the sky, cast a strange glow over the wide, desolate marshes. A mile back rose the dark line of the uplands, with small, white farmhouses already hidden in shadow.

Captain Joe Boultbee had just left his wagon standing in the dike road, with his four-year-old boy on the seat. He was on the point of crossing the dike, to visit the little landing-place where he kept his boat, when above the rush and whistle of

"HOW THE WIND ROARED IN FROM THE SEA!"

the gale he heard Jamie's voice. He
hurried back a few paces before he
could make out what the little fellow
was saying.

Captain Joe and Jamie

"Pap," cried the child, "I want to get out of the wagon. 'Fraid Bill goin' to run away!"

"Oh, nonsense!" answered Captain Joe. "Bill won't run away. He doesn't know how. You stay there, and don't be frightened, and I'll be right back."

"But, pap, the wind blows me too hard," piped the small voice, pleadingly.

"Oh, all right," said the father, and returning to the wagon he lifted the child gently down and set him on his feet. "Now," he continued, "it's too windy for you out on the other side of the dike. You run over and sit on that big stick, where the wind can't get at you; and wait for me. And be sure you don't let Bill run away."

Captain Joe and Jamie

As he spoke the Captain noticed that the horse, ordinarily one of the most stolid of creatures, seemed tonight peculiarly uneasy; with his head up in the air he was sniffing nervously, and glancing from side to side. As Jamie was trudging through the long grass to the seat which his father had shown him, the Captain said, "Why, Bill *does* seem scary, after all; who'd have thought this wind would scare *him?*"

"Bill don't like it," replied Jamie; "it blows him too hard." And, glad to be out of the gale, which took his breath away, the little fellow seated himself contentedly in the shelter of the dike. Just then there was a clatter of wheels and a crash. Bill had whirled sharply about in the narrow road, upsetting and smashing the light wagon.

Now, utterly heedless of his master's angry shouts, he was galloping in mad haste back toward the uplands, with the fragments of the wagon at his heels. The Captain and Jamie watched him flying before the wind, a red spectre in the lurid light. Then, turning away once more to see to his boat, the Captain remarked, "Well, laddie, I guess we'll have to foot it back when we get through here. But Bill's going to have a licking for this!"

Captain Joe and Jamie

Left to himself, Jamie crouched down behind the dike, a strange, solitary little figure in the wide waste of the marshes. Though the full force of the gale could not reach him, his long fair curls were blown across his face, and he clung determinedly to his small, round hat. For a while he watched the beam of red light, till the jagged fringe of clouds closed over it, and it was gone. Then, in the dusk, he began to feel a little frightened; but he knew his father would soon be back, and he did n't like to call him again.

Captain Joe and Jamie He listened to the waves washing, surging, beating, roaring, on the shoals beyond the dike. Presently he heard them, every now and then, thunder in against the very dike itself. Upon this he grew more frightened, and called to his father several times. But of course the small voice was drowned in the tumult of wind and wave, and the father, working eagerly on the other side of the dike, heard no sound of it.

Close by the shelter in which Jamie was crouching there were several great tubs, made by sawing molasses-hogsheads into halves. These tubs, in fishing season, were carried by the fishermen in their boats, to hold the shad as they were taken from the net. Now they stood empty and dry, but highly flavored with memories of their office. Into the nearest tub Jamie crawled, after having shouted in vain to his father.

To the child's loneliness and fear *Captain* the tub looked "cosey," as he called *Joe and* it. He curled up in the bottom, *Jamie* and felt a little comforted.

Jamie was the only child of Captain Joe Boultbee. When Jamie was about two years old, the Captain had taken the child and his mother on a voyage to Brazil. While calling at Barbadoes the young mother had caught the yellow fever. There she had died, and was buried. After that voyage Captain Joe had given up his ship, and retired to his father's farm at Tantramar. There he devoted himself to Jamie and the farm, but to Jamie especially; and in the summer, partly for amusement, partly for profit, he was accustomed to spend a few weeks in drifting for shad on the wild tides of Chignecto Bay. Wherever he went, Jamie went. If the weather was too rough for Jamie, Captain Joe stayed at home. As for the

Captain Joe and Jamie child, petted without being spoiled, he was growing a tough and manly little soul, and daily more and more the delight of his father's heart.

Why should he leave him curled up in his tub on the edge of the marshes, on a night so wild? In truth, though the wind was tremendous, and now growing to a veritable hurricane, there was no apparent danger or great hardship on the marshes. It was not cold, and there was no rain.

Captain Joe, foreseeing a heavy gale, together with a tide higher than usual, had driven over to the dike to make his little craft more secure.

He found the boat already in confusion; and the wind, when once he had crossed out of the dike's shelter, was so much more violent than he had expected, that it took him some time to get things "snugged up." He felt that Jamie was all right, as long as he was out of the wind. He was only a stone's throw distant, though hidden by the great rampart of the dike. But the Captain began to wish that he had left the little fellow at home, as he knew the long walk over the rough road, in the dark and the furious gale, would sorely tire the sturdy little legs. Every now and then, as vigorously and cheerfully he worked in the pitching smack, the Captain sent a shout of greeting over the dike to keep the little lad from getting lonely. But the storm blew his voice far up into the clouds, and Jamie, in his tub, never heard it.

By the time Captain Joe had put everything shipshape, he noticed that his plunging boat had drifted close to the dike. He had never before seen the tide reach such a height. The waves that were rocking the little craft so violently, were a mere back-wash from the great seas which, as he now observed with a pang,

Captain Joe and Jamie were thundering in a little further up the coast. Just at this spot the dike was protected from the full force of the storm by Snowdons' Point. "What if the dike should break up yonder, and this fearful tide get in on the marshes?" thought the Captain, in a sudden anguish of apprehension. Leaving the boat to dash itself to pieces if it liked, he clambered in breathless haste out on to the top of the dike, shouting to Jamie as he did so. There was no answer. Where he had left the little one but a half-hour back, the tide was seething three or four feet deep over the grasses.

Dark as the night had grown, it grew blacker before the father's eyes. For an instant his heart stood still with horror, then he sprang down into the flood. The water boiled up nearly to his arm-pits. With his feet he felt the great timber, fastened in the dike, on which his boy had been sitting. He peered through the dark, with straining eyes grown preternaturally keen. He could see nothing on the wide, swirling surface save two or three dark objects, far out in the marsh. These he recognized at once as his fish-tubs gone afloat. Then he ran up the dike toward the Point. "Surely," he groaned in his heart, "Jamie has climbed up the dike when he saw the water coming, and I'll find him along the top here, somewhere, looking and crying for me!"

Captain Joe and Jamie

Then, running like a madman along the narrow summit, with a band of iron tightening about his heart, the Captain reached the Point, where the dike took its beginning.

No sign of the little one; but he saw the marshes everywhere laid waste. Then he turned round and sped back, thinking perhaps Jamie had wandered in the other direction. Passing the now buried landing-

Captain Joe and Jamie place, he saw with a curious distinctness, as if in a picture, that the boat was turned bottom up, and glued to the side of the dike.

Suddenly he checked his speed with a violent effort, and threw himself upon his face, clutching the short grasses of the dike. He had just saved himself from falling into the sea. Had he had time to think, he might not have tried to save himself, believing as he did that the child who was his very life had perished. But the instinct of self-preservation had asserted itself blindly, and just in time. Before his feet the dike was washed away, and through the chasm the waves were breaking furiously.

Meanwhile, what had become of Jamie?

The wind had made him drowsy, and before he had been many minutes curled up in the tub, he was sound asleep.

When the dike gave way, some

distance from Jamie's queer retreat, there came suddenly a great rush of water among the tubs, and some were straightway floated off. Then others a little heavier followed, one by one; and, last of all, the heaviest, that containing Jamie and his fortunes. The water rose rapidly, but back here there came no waves, and the child slept as peacefully as if at home in his crib. Little the Captain thought, when his eyes wandered over the floating tubs, that the one nearest to him was freighted with his heart's treasure! And well it was that Jamie did not hear his shouts and wake! Had he done so, he would have at once sprung to his feet and been tipped out into the flood.

Captain Joe and Jamie

By this time the great tide had reached its height. Soon it began to recede, but slowly, for the storm kept the waters gathered, as it were, into a heap at the head of the bay.

Captain Joe and Jamie

All night the wind raged on, wrecking the smacks and schooners along the coast, breaking down the dikes in a hundred places, flooding all the marshes, and drowning many cattle in the salt pastures. All night the Captain, hopeless and mute in his agony of grief, lay clutching the grasses on the dike-top, not noticing when at length the waves ceased to drench him with their spray. All night, too, slept Jamie in his tub.

Right across the marsh the strange craft drifted before the wind, never getting into the region where the waves were violent. Such motion as there was — and at times it was somewhat lively — seemed only to lull the child to a sounder slumber. Toward daybreak the tub grounded at the foot of the uplands, not far from the edge of the road. The waters gradually slunk away, as if ashamed of their wild vagaries. And still the child slept on.

As the light broke over the bay, *Captain* coldly pink and desolately gleaming, *Joe and* Captain Joe got up and looked about *Jamie* him. His eyes were tearless, but his face was gray and hard, and deep lines had stamped themselves across it during the night.

Seeing that the marshes were again uncovered, save for great shallow pools left here and there, he set out to find the body of his boy. After wandering aimlessly for perhaps an hour, the Captain began to study the direction in which the wind had been blowing. This was almost exactly with the road which led to his home on the uplands. As he noticed this, a wave of pity crossed his heart, at thought of the terrible anxiety his father and mother had all that night been enduring. Then in an instant there seemed to unroll before him the long, slow years of the desolation of that home without Jamie.

All this time he was moving along

Captain Joe and Jamie the soaked road, scanning the marsh in every direction. When he had covered about half the distance, he was aware of his father, hastening with feeble eagerness to meet him.

The night of watching had made the old man haggard, but his face lit up at sight of his son. As he drew near, however, and saw no sign of Jamie, and marked the look upon the Captain's face, the gladness died out as quickly as it had come. When the two men met, the elder put out his hand in silence, and the younger clasped it. There was no room for words. Side by side the two walked slowly homeward. With restless eyes, ever dreading lest they should find that which they sought, the father and son looked everywhere, — except in a certain old fish-tub which they passed. The tub stood a little to one side of the road. Just at this time a sparrow lit on the tub's edge, and uttered a loud and startled chirp at sight of the sleeping child. As the bird flew off precipitately, Jamie opened his eyes, and gazed up in astonishment at the blue sky over his head. He stretched out his hand and felt the rough sides of the tub. Then, in complete bewilderment, he clambered to his feet. Why, there was his father, walking away somewhere without him! And grandpapa, too! Jamie felt aggrieved.

"Pap!" he cried, in a loud but tearful voice, "where you goin' to?"

A great wave of light seemed to break across the landscape, as the two men turned and saw the little golden head shining, dishevelled, over the edge of the tub. The Captain caught his breath with a sort of sob, and rushed to snatch the little one in his arms; while the grandfather fell on his knees in the road, and his trembling lips moved silently.

The Barn on the Marsh.

It had not always stood on the marsh. When I was a little boy of seven, it occupied the rear of our neighbor's yard, not a stone's throw from the rectory gate, on one of the windy, sunshiny spurs of South Mountain. A perpetual eyesore to the rector; but I cannot help thinking, as I view it now in the concentrated light of memory, that it did artistic service in the way of a foil to the loveliness of the rectory garden. This garden was the rector's delight, but to my restless seven years it was a sort of gay-colored and ever-threatening bugbear.

Weeding, and especially such thorough, radical weeding as alone would satisfy the rector's conscience, was my detestation; and, moreover, just at the time of being called upon to weed, there was sure to be something else of engrossing importance which my nimble little wits had set themselves upon doing.

But I never found courage to betray my lack of sympathy in all its iciness. The sight of the rector's enthusiasm filled me ever with a sense of guilt, and I used to weed quite diligently, at times.

One morning the rector had lured me out early, before breakfast, while the sun yet hung low above the shining marshes. We were working cheerfully together at the carrot-beds. The smell of the moist earth and of the dewy young carrot-plants, bruised by my hasty fingers, comes vividly upon my senses even now.

The Barn on the Marsh

Suddenly I heard the rector cry, "Bother!" in a tone which spoke volumes. I saw he had broken his hoe short off at the handle. I stopped work with alacrity, and gazed with commiserating interest, while I began wiping my muddy little fingers on my knickerbockers in bright anticipation of some new departure which should put a pause to the weeding.

In a moment or two the vexed wrinkles smoothed themselves out of the rector's brow, and he turned to me with the proposal that we should go over to our neighbor's and repair the damage.

One end of the barn, as we knew, was used for a workshop. We crossed the road, let down the bars, put to flight a flock of pigeons that were feeding among the scattered straw, and threw open the big barn doors.

There, just inside, hung the dead

"THERE, HUNG THE DEAD BODY OF OUR NEIGHBOR."

body of our neighbor, his face distorted and purple. And, while I stood sobbing with horror, the rector cut him down with the drawknife which he had come to borrow.

Soon after this tragedy, the barn was moved down to the marsh, to be used for storing hay and farm implements. And by the time the scene had faded from my mind, the rector gave up the dear delights of his garden, and took us off to a distant city parish. Not until I had reached eighteen, and the dignity of college cap and gown, did I revisit the salty breezes of South Mountain.

Then I came to see friends who were living in the old rectory. About two miles away, by the main road, dwelt certain other friends, with whom I was given to spending most of my evenings, and who possessed some strange charm which would never permit me to say good-night at anything like a seasonable hour.

The Barn on the Marsh

The distance, as I said, to these friends was about two miles, if you followed the main road; but there was a short cut, a road across the marsh, used chiefly by the hay-makers and the fishermen, not pleasant to travel in wet weather, but good enough for me at all times in the frame of mind in which I found myself.

This road, on either hand, was bordered by a high rail fence, along which rose, here and there, the bleak spire of a ghostly and perishing Lombardy poplar. This is the tree of all least suited to those wind-beaten regions, but none other will the country people plant. Close up to the road, at one point, curved a massive sweep of red dike, and further to the right stretched the miles on miles of naked marsh, till they lost themselves in the lonely, shifting waters of the Basin.

About twenty paces back from the fence, with its big doors opening toward the road, a conspicuous landmark in all my nightly walks, stood the barn.

The Barn on the Marsh

I remembered vividly enough, but in a remote, impersonal sort of way, the scene on that far-off sunny summer morning. As, night after night, I swung past the ancient doors, my brain in a pleasant confusion, I never gave the remembrance any heed. Finally, I ceased to recall it, and the rattling of the wind in the time-warped shingles fell on utterly careless ears.

One night, as I started homeward upon the verge of twelve, the marsh seemed all alive with flying gleams. The moon was past the full, white and high; the sky was thick with small black clouds, streaming dizzily across the moon's face, and a moist wind piped steadily in from the sea.

I was walking swiftly, not much alive to outward impressions, scarce

The Barn on the Marsh noticing even the strange play of the moon-shadows over the marshes, and had got perhaps a stone's throw past the barn, when a creeping sensation about my skin, and a thrill of nervous apprehension made me stop suddenly and take a look behind.

The impulse seized me unawares, or I should have laughed at myself and gone on without yielding to such a weakness. But it was too late. My gaze darted unerringly to the barn, whose great doors stood wide open. There, swaying almost imperceptibly in the wind, hung the body of our neighbor, as I had seen it that dreadful morning long ago.

For a moment I could hear again my childish sobs, and the remembrance of that horror filled me with self-pity. Then, as the roots of my hair began to stir, my feet set themselves instinctively for flight. This instinct, however, I promptly and sternly repressed. I knew all about these optical illusions, and tried to congratulate myself on this opportunity for investigating one so interesting and vivid. At the same time I gave a hasty side-thought to what would have happened had I been one of the superstitious farm-hands or fishermen of the district. I should have taken to my heels in desperate terror, and been ever after faithfully persuaded of having looked upon a veritable ghost.

I said to myself that the apparition, if I looked upon it steadfastly, would vanish as I approached, or, more probably, resolve itself into some chance combination of moonlight and shadows. In fact, my reason was perfectly satisfied that the ghostly vision was due solely to the association of ideas, — I was fresh from my classes in philosophy, — aided and abetted by my own pretty vivid imagination. Yet the natural man, this physical being of mine,

The Barn on the Marsh revolted in every fibre of the flesh from any closer acquaintance with the thing.

I began, with reluctant feet, to retrace my steps; but as I did so, the vision only grew so much the clearer; and a cold perspiration broke out upon me. Step by step I approached, till I stood just outside the fence, face to face with the apparition.

I leaned against the fence, looking through between the rails; and now, at this distance, every feature came out with awful distinctness — all so horrible in its distortion that I cannot bear to describe it.

As each fresh gust of wind hissed through the chinks, I could see the body swing before it, heavily and slowly. I had to bring all my philosophy to bear, else my feet would have carried me off in a frenzy of flight.

At last I reached the conclusion that since my sight was so helplessly deceived, I should have to depend upon the touch. In no other way could I detect the true basis of the illusion; and this way was a hard one. By much argument and self-persuasion I prevailed upon myself to climb the fence, and with a sort of despairing doggedness to let myself down on the inside.

Just then the clouds thickened over the face of the moon, and the light faded rapidly. To get down inside the fence with that thing was, for a moment, simply sickening, and my eyes dilated with the intensity of my stare. Then common-sense came to the rescue, with a revulsion of feeling, and I laughed — though not very mirthfully — at the thoroughness of my scare.

With an assumption of coolness and defiance I walked right up to the open doors; and when so close that I could have touched it with my walking-stick, the thing swayed

The Barn on the Marsh gently and faced me in the light of the re-appearing moon.

Could my eyes deceive me? It certainly was our neighbor.

Scarcely knowing what I did, I thrust out my stick and touched it, shrinking back as I did so. What I touched, plain instantly to my sight, was a piece of wood and iron, —some portion of a mowing-machine or reaper, which had been, apparently, repainted and hung up across the door-pole to dry.

It swayed in the wind. The straying fingers of the moonbeams through the chinks pencilled it strangely, and the shadows were huddled black behind it. But now it hung revealed, with no more likeness to a human body than any average well-meaning farm-implement might be expected to have.

With a huge sigh of relief I turned away. As I climbed the fence once more I gave a parting glance toward

the yawning doorway of the barn on *The Barn*
the marsh. There, as plain as before *on the*
I had pierced the bubble, swung the *Marsh*
body of my neighbor. And all the
way home, though I would not turn
my head, I felt it at my heels.

The Stone Dog.

IT was drawing towards sunset, and I had reached the outskirts of the city, which here came to an abrupt end upon the very edge of the marshes. The marshes stretched before me bare and gray, with here and there a flush of evening color, serving but to emphasize their utterness of desolation. Here and there, also, lay broad pools, their shore and water gradually intermerging through a sullen fringe of reeds. The river, which had been my day-long companion — a noisy stream flowing through breezy hills, and villages, and vineyards — having loitered to draw its circle about the city walls, had fallen under a spell. It met me here a featureless, brimming ditch, and wound away in torpid coils to the monotonous horizon. And now this shrunken city, its edges dead and fallen to decay, these naked levels, where not even a bittern's voice had courage to startle the stillness, filled me, in spite of myself, with a vague apprehensiveness. Just as one who is groping in profound darkness feels his eyes dilate in the effort to catch the least glimmer of light, I found my senses all on the strain, attentive to their very utmost. Though the atmosphere was heavy and deadening, my eyes were so watchful that not even the uprising of some weeds, trodden down, perhaps, hours before by a passing foot, escaped their notice. My nostrils were keenly conscious of the sick metallic odor from the marshes, of the pleasanter perfume of dry reed panicles, of the chill, damp smell of mouldering

The stone-work, and of a strangely dis-
Stone Dog agreeable haunting essence from a certain dull-colored weed, whose leaves, which shot up within tempting reach of my hand, I had idly bruised in passing. My ears, for all their painful expectancy, heard at first no sound save the rustle of a frightened mouse in the dead grass near; but at length they detected the gurgle of running water, made audible by a faint stray wind which breathed in my direction.

Instinctively I turned and followed the sound. On my right a huge fragment of the wall jutted into the marsh, and passing this I saw before me, brightened by the sunset, a narrow stretch of dry, baked soil, raised somewhat above the level of the pools, and strewn with shattered bricks and scraps of tiling and potsherds. The musical lapsing of the water now fell upon my ears distinctly, and I saw a little way off a quaint old fountain, standing half a stonecast clear of the wall. With the sunlight bathing it, the limpid water sparkling away from its base, it was the only cheerful object in the landscape; yet I felt an unaccountable reluctance to approach it. The evil enchantment which seemed to brood over the place, the weird fantasies chasing each other through my unconsenting brain, annoyed me greatly, for I profess to hold my imagination pretty well under control, and to have but small concern for ghostly horrors. Shaking aside my nervousness, I began to whistle softly as I strolled up to examine the old fountain. But on noticing how lugubrious, how appropriate to the neighborhood and my feelings was the air that came to my lips, I laughed aloud. At the sudden sound of my voice I felt both startled and somewhat abashed. Laughter here was clearly out of place; and besides,

The Stone Dog the echo that followed was obtrusively and unpleasantly distinct, appearing to come both from a deep-arched doorway in the wall near by, and from the vaulted hollow of the basin of the fount, which lay just beneath the dog's jaws. As I should have said before, the fountain was a great cube of darkish stone, along the top of which a stone dog crouched; and the water gushed from between its carved fore-paws into a deep basin, the side of which was cleft two thirds of the way to its base. Through this break, which I saw to be an old one from the layers of green film lining it, the stream bubbled out and ran off among barren heaps of débris, to sink itself in the weeds of some stagnant pool. The head of the dog was thrust forward and rested upon the fore-paws as if the brute were sleeping; but its half-open eyes seemed to watch the approaches to the doorway in the wall. As a piece of sculpture, the animal was simply *The* marvellous. In its gathered limbs, *Stone Dog* though relaxed and perfectly at rest, a capacity for swift and terrible action seemed to hold itself in reserve, and a breath almost appeared to come from the half-opened jaws, momentarily dimming the crystal that smoothly gushed beneath. No scrap of vegetation could the rill persuade out of the inexorable sterility around, saving for some curdled greenish mosses that waved slowly from the sides of the basin, or pointed from roothold on brick and shard, where the small current loitered a little. I am not a taker of notes, nor, for all my vagrant and exploring tendencies, am I a very close observer. Nevertheless, though it is now a year and a half since what I am telling of took place, the minutest details of that strange fountain, and of the scene about it, are as definitely before me as if I had been there but yesterday. I am not

The Stone Dog going to inflict them all upon my reader, yet would do so without a spark of compunction, if by such means I could dim the all too vivid remembrance. The experiences that befell me by this fountain have shaken painfully the confidence I once enjoyed as to the fulness of my knowledge of the powers of things material. I cannot say that I have become credulous; but I have ceased to regard as necessarily absurd whatever I find it difficult to explain.

From the fountain it was not a score of paces to the doorway in the wall, which was sunk below the surface of the ground, so that the crumbling arch surmounting it was scarcely on a level with my feet. Steep narrow stairs of brick work, consisting, I think, of seven steps, led down to it. The doorway had once been elaborately ornamented with mouldings in yellow stucco, most of which had fallen, and all but choked the stairs. The crude pale color of these *The* fragments jarred harshly against the *Stone Dog* olive of the damp stone foundations and the stained brown of the mouldy brick. After my usual fashion, I set myself to explore this doorway, in my interest half forgetting my apprehensions. As I descended the steps the sound of the running water faded out, with a suddenness which caught my ear, though failing to fix my attention. But as I made to grasp the great rusty iron doorhandle, which was curiously wrought of two dragons intertwisted neck and tail, again my every sense sprang on the alert, and a chill of terror crept tingling through my frame. My straining ears could detect not the slightest sound from the fountain, which was within plain view behind me. I felt as if some eye were fixed upon me. I faced sharply about and set foot on the steps to ascend. And I saw the water at that very moment

The Stone Dog burst forth afresh between the feet of the dog, from whose eye a dull white glow seemed just vanishing. It must be borne in mind that the beast's flank was toward the doorway, and, in consequence, only one of its half-closed eyes visible from where I stood. I ascended and went straight to the fountain. I grasped the great stone head and gave it a wrench, but found it just as immovable as it looked. Vexed at my idiotic fears, I vowed to take my fill of investigating that doorway, and to find out if there lay anything of interest beyond it. I knew this part of the city was quite deserted, and that no outraged householder in the flesh was likely to confront my trespassings. But the last of the daylight was now upon me, and I thought best to postpone my enterprise till the morrow. As I betook myself back toward humanity and lodgings, I felt that eye piercing me

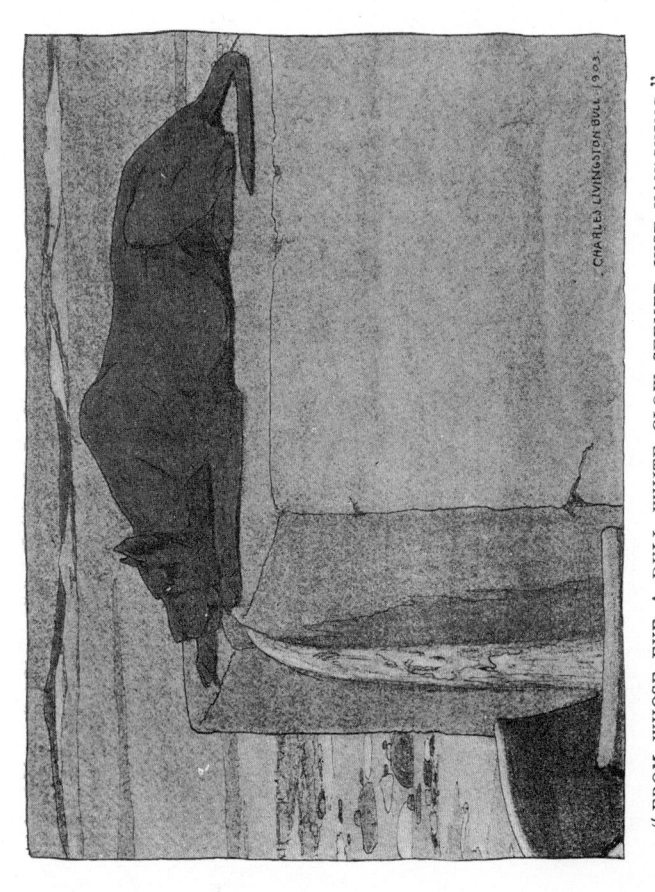

"FROM WHOSE EYE A DULL WHITE GLOW SEEMED JUST VANISHING."

till I rounded the buttress of the wall; but I denied my folly permission to look back.

The following morning was spent among the curious old cafés, the unexpected squares, and the gorgeous but dilapidated churches of the inhabited city. All these things, however, failed to interest me. With more time on my hands than I quite knew what to do with, I yet felt as if my time were being wasted. The spell of the dead outskirts, of the shadowless dead marshes, of that mysterious and inscrutable dog, clung to me with unrelenting persistence. And the early afternoon found me standing again by the fountain.

Familiarly I scooped up the cool water and drank it from my palm. I scattered it over the parched bricks and clay, which instantly soaked it in. I dashed a few drops also, playfully, upon the image of the dog, which had taken, the evening be-

The Stone Dog fore, such fantastic liberties with my overwrought fancy. But these drops gathered themselves up nimbly into little shining balls, and fled off to the ground like so much quicksilver. I looked out upon the wan pools and marshes, whence a greenish mist steamed up, and seemed to poison the sunlight streaming through it. It is possible that this semblance of an unwholesome mist was not so much the fault of the marshes as a condition of the atmosphere, premonitory of the fierce electric storms and the earthquake which visited the city that same night. The greenish light beat full on the sunken doorway, so that only the lowermost steps remained in shadow. However unattractive the temporary complexion of the sun, I was glad of his company as I descended the steps. The twisting dragons of the doorhandle attracted me as I drew near. As for the dog, I had exorcised it from my imagination with those nimble drops of water; and for the old door, it looked as if a little persuasion would make it yield whatever secret it might chance to have in keeping. But certainly, if I might credit my ears, which had once more grown abnormally attentive, the sound of the water had ceased. My flesh began to creep a little, though I told myself the fading of the sound was entirely due to my position, — that the walls of the stairway intercepted it. At the same time I felt that eye watching me, and a chilly sweat broke out upon my limbs; but I execrated my folly, and refused to turn my head. Meanwhile, so alert had become my hearing that the escape of some gases, bubbling up from the bottom of a pool far out in the marsh, resounded as if close beside me. I tried to force the bolt back, but in vain; and I had just come to the conclusion that a sharp wrench

The Stone Dog would break away bolt, socket, and all, when an uncontrollable instinct of fear turned me about to see what peril threatened. The head of the dog was facing directly toward me, and its eyes, now wide open, flamed upon me with strange and awful whiteness. I sprang up the steps and was at the beast's side in an instant; but I found the head, as before, resting upon the paws, the eyes half closed and dull, the water gushing down into the basin.

As I bathed my shaking hands and clammy forehead, I laughed with deep irritation. I said then to myself that the ignorant could hardly be blamed for even the wildest superstitions, when a cool-headed and enlightened modern like myself was so wrought upon by the fictions of his brain. I philosophized for some time, however, before I got the better of my repugnance to that doorway. I humorously assured myself

that, at the worst, this incompre- *The*
hensible beast was securely anchored *Stone Dog*
to his fountain; and that if anything
terrible were at the other side of the
door which I was going to open, it
surely could not be capable of much,
good or ill, after its century or so
of imprisonment. Then I walked
firmly straight to the doorway and
down the seven steps; and I knew
that first one eye was turned upon
me, then both; the water was silent
before I had gone ten paces.

It was useless trying to conquer
the creeping of my skin, the fear that
pricked along my nerves; so, bidding my reason ignore these minor
discomforts, I busied myself with
the problem of loosening the bolt-socket. It occurred to me at the
time that there might be an easier
entrance at the other side of the wall,
as nothing in this neighborhood was
in good enough repair to boast of
more than three walls standing; but

The Stone Dog no, that would have been a concession to my illusions. I chipped away at the soft stone with my knife. I jerked hard upon the bolt, which gave a little, with clatter of falling stucco; and on the instant I faced around like lightning, in an indescribable horror. There, at the very top of the steps, crouched the dog, its head thrust down close to my face. The stone jaws were grinning apart. A most appalling menace was in the wide, white eyes. I know I tugged once more upon the bolt, for a great piece of the door and arch crumbled and came away; and I thought, as the head closed down, that I made a wild spring to get past the crouching form. Then reason and consciousness forsook me.

When sense returned, I found myself lying on a pile of rags, in a darkish, garlicky hut, with the morning sunlight streaming in through the open door. I sat up, with the memory of my horror vivid upon me, and wondered, with a sigh of relief at the change, what sort of a place I had got to. I was in a very different quarter of the city from the neighborhood of the fountain. Here were still the ruined outskirts, still the desolate marshes, but the highlands backing the city on the north began to rise just beyond the hut's door. I got up, but found my right shoulder almost disabled. I could not lift my arm without great pain. Yet my clothing was not torn, and bore no marks save of dust and travel. I was about to uncover and examine the damaged shoulder, when in came the owner of the hut, an honest-looking, heavy-set muleteer, who showed all his teeth in his gratification at observing my recovery.

As I gathered from my host, he had had occasion to pass what he called the "Fonte del Cano" near sunset of the afternoon preceding.

The Stone Dog He had found me lying in a stupor, face down, across the basin of the fount, and directly beneath the jaws of the dog, which he piously crossed himself on mentioning. Not stopping to look for explanations, though he saw the old door was partly broken away, he had put me on his mule and made haste homeward, in fear of the coming of twilight in that grim place. There had come up a great storm in the night, and then an earthquake, shaking down many old walls that had long been toppling to their fall. After sunrise, being a bold fellow, he had gone again to the place, in hope of finding some treasure revealed by the disturbance. Report said there was treasure of some kind hidden within the wall; but none had dared to look for it since the day, years before his birth, when two men undertaking the search had gone mad, with the great white eyes of the dog turned terribly upon them. There were other strange *The Stone Dog* things said about the spot, he acknowledged reluctantly, which, however, he would not talk of even in daylight; and for himself, in truth, he knew but little of them. Now, he continued, in place of anything having been laid bare, the whole top of the wall had fallen down and buried steps and doorway in masses of ruin. But the fountain and the dog were untouched, and he had not cared to go nearer than was necessary.

Having reached my lodgings, I rewarded the honest fellow and sent him away in high feather, all-forgetful of the treasure which the earthquake had failed to unearth for him. Once alone in my room, I made haste to examine my shoulder. I found it green and livid. I found also, with a sick feeling which I shall not soon forget, that it was bruised on either side with deep prints of massive teeth.

Stony - Lonesome.

LYDIA's eyes strayed over the wide, wooded valley, over the far-off rim of purple hills, and rested wistfully on the tremulous blue beyond. She laid her arms along the top of the worn gray bars, and leaned her rosy face upon her folded brown hands, and fetched a long sigh from the very bottom of her heart. And still she kept her eyes fixed on that patch of shimmering sky. How well she knew that spot, set apart from all the rest of the spacious empty heavens by two jutting shoulders of the hills! In that high notch the sky seemed, to Lydia, ever intenser and more mysterious than elsewhere. It was of a deeper, more palpitating blueness there in the dew-washed summer mornings, of a more thrilling opalescence in the hazy, heated noons, of a more ineffable golden translucency after the setting of the sun. Even at night, too, the place was marked out for her, a low star sometimes beaming like a beacon through the notch.

Stony-Lonesome

Presently the girl lifted her head, and impatiently threw back a loose wisp of crinkled gold-brown hair. Then she dashed a tear from her cheek.

"I wish, oh, I wish as how I could go! If only gran'mother an' gran'dad could git along without me for a spell!"

She turned, picked up her two pails, each half-full of water from the spring, and started up the long, stony lane toward the house. A strong wooden hoop, once part of a

[251]

Stony-Lonesome molasses hogshead, encircling her a little above the knees, kept the pails from striking against her as she walked. She stepped with resolute alertness, and would not let herself look back toward that magic spot of sky. Her work at the house was calling for her.

Somewhere far beyond that spot of sky, according to her painstaking calculations and much eager study of the maps in her school geography, lay the city of Lydia's dreams. From early childhood she had heard and read of Boston, and longed for it. Girls whom she knew, her schoolmates, shy, shabby, and awkward, had gone thither, to disappear from her view for a year or two. They had returned in glorious apparel, self-confident and glib of tongue, to dazzle down all criticism in their quiet Nova Scotian backwoods settlement. Their visits were always brief, but they left heart-burnings and discontent behind them. Lydia had it in her mind that she would never learn those bold glances and that loud chattering in Boston, but her imagination was all on fire with dreams and ambitions, which in Boston only, she thought, could ever find fulfilment. It was not lack of money that kept her, chained and fretting, on the old farm of Stony-Lonesome, as John Cassidy's place was called. She would have borrowed the little necessary cash, strong in the faith that she would be able to pay it back when she got to the Eldorado of her desires. But her grandfather and grandmother were getting old, and she was all they had to make life sweet. She felt that she was bound to stay at home. Over and over again, as she sent her very soul out toward that mysterious patch of sky, Lydia told herself that she could not purchase the satisfaction of her desire at the cost of lone-

Stony-Lonesome liness and sorrow for the old people. But the longing in her vigorous young heart grew daily more hard to resist, while her wrestlings with the tyrannous impulse grew daily more feeble. She began to feel with remorse the approach of a day when she would be no longer able to sustain the unequal contest.

It was with a very anguish of apprehension that Lydia's grandparents watched her growing restlessness. Their fear was no mere selfish passion. The grandmother, indeed, a gentle, motherly woman, would sit rocking in the sunny porch, and thinking, thinking, thinking, of what Stony-Lonesome would be without "Lyddy." Far worse than this, to John Cassidy, was a black horror of Boston, which lay like a nightmare on his soul. He loved Lydia with all the pent-up force of a grim, undemonstrative nature; yet the thought of his own pain at losing the sunshine of her presence hardly touched him. His dreams were racked with visions of Lydia's ruin. He had never seen a city; and he had imagination. In his eyes Boston was a sort of Babylon, where Vice, in grotesquely leering shapes (fashioned from boyish memories of an illustrated copy of the " Pilgrim's Progress"), caught openly in the streets at the white skirts of Innocence.

Lydia knew that her grandfather hated Boston with a hate that would endure no argument; and she knew that her grandmother also trembled at the name. The reason for this, however, was far indeed from her remotest guess. The old, old tragedy was at the foundation of it. Lydia's mother, grown heartsick at eighteen with the bright desolation of Stony-Lonesome, had shaken off restraint and fled away to Boston. After two years at service there she had come back to Stony-Lonesome, broken

Stony-Lonesome with pain and shame, deserted by a false lover. Her mother, taking her back to her aching heart, had striven to comfort her; but her father, for three long, bitter months, had held sternly aloof from her contrition. Then, forgiving her upon her deathbed, in an agony of love and grief which she had pitifully tried to soothe, he had taken her child to his heart with a consuming devotion. To him, thenceforth, life found expression only in terms of Lydia. This was the name her dying mother had bestowed upon the child, and this, without abbreviation, John Cassidy had called her from the cradle; but the grandmother had shortened it to "Lyddy."

As for the name "Stony-Lonesome," never was appellation more apt. John Cassidy's father, an eccentric recluse, had built his house upon a hill on the remotest edge of Brine Settlement. The farm had

good land attached to it, in the adja- *Stony-*
cent valley; but the long, round hill, *Lonesome*
licked naked by an ancient conflagration, was of niggard soil and thick-sown with granite boulders. The house was built so well that time appeared unwilling to try conclusions with it, and so warmly that its occupants did not suffer from its bleak situation. Low-walled and wide, rain-washed to a gray which blended with the surrounding stones, it seemed an outgrowth of the hill itself. The front door was dull yellow. At one corner arose, like a steeple, the stiff gray form of a Lombardy poplar, the only tree on the hill. At the other corner, where the ell straggled off leanly from the main house, stood a huge hogshead to catch the rain-water from the roof. A little square of garden, sloping from the front door, and fenced with low walls of stones carefully piled, was bright with sweet-william and bachelor's-

Stony-Lonesome button and phlox. This patch of color took on a curious pathos from the wide severity which it so vainly strove to soften. The ample barns, which as a rule succeed in giving a certain kindly air to the bleakest scene, were hidden behind the house at Stony-Lonesome.

As Lydia, gracefully and steadily carrying her two pails of water, reached the top of the hill and turned the corner toward the kitchen door, John Cassidy lifted his eyes from his corn-hoeing in the lower field. He saw Lydia pause at the corner of the house and cast one lingering backward look across the valley toward that notch in the hills. He had watched her at this before, and had come to know what it meant. He trembled, and muttered to himself, "She's got it! The p'ison's workin' in her blood! That's what's makin' her fret so, longin' to be away to that hell on earth. Lydia, Lydia, I'd ruther see your dear young eyes shet white an' fast in death than see ye go like your poor mother done!"

Stony-Lonesome

Then, with knit brows and set lips, he went on with his hoeing, till presently Lydia appeared in the kitchen door and blew a long, echoing note on the great shell which served as a dinner-horn. John Cassidy straightened his back, threw down the hoe, and started for the house; and the hired man appeared, coming from behind a copse further down the valley.

The hired man sat down at the dinner-table along with Mr. and Mrs. Cassidy and Lydia. His name was Job. A pair of kind but shrewd blue eyes twinkled under his pale and bushy eyebrows, giving an alert look to his otherwise heavy face, which was round, red, and hairless. After shovelling a huge quantity of fish and potatoes into his mouth,

Stony-Lonesome using his knife for the purpose, he stopped for breath.

"Jim Ed Barnes come by as I was workin' in the back lot this forenoon," said he.

"What did Jim Ed have to say for himself?" asked Lydia.

"He was tellin' me," answered Job, "how fine his sister Ellen was hittin' it off in Bawston."

Mr. and Mrs. Cassidy looked at each other. The old man's face paled slightly, while his wife made a hasty effort to change the subject.

"Did he say how his mother's leg was gittin'?" she inquired, with an excellent assumption of eagerness on her large, gentle face.

But Lydia interrupted. "What's she doing, Job? And how is she gitting along? And how does she like it in Bawston?" she queried breathlessly.

"Why," said Job, "she's got to be forewoman in a big millin'ry store.

She was always neat-fingered, y' know, an' took natural to that kinder thing. An' now she's makin' money, I reckon! Why, Jim Ed says as how she sent home two hundred dollars yesterday, to help pay off the mortgage on their place."

Stony-Lonesome

The potato which he was eating became to John Cassidy as dry as sawdust, and stuck in his throat. He heard Lydia burst out with the cry he had so long been dreading.

"Oh, gran'dad, oh, gran'mother," she pleaded, "if only I could go for a little spell an' try it! I know I could do well, — I feel it in me, — an' I'd so love to help you pay off that mortgage on Stony-Lonesome that gives you so much bother every year!"

Seeing their faces of denial, she would not give them time to speak, but went on hastily: "An' I'd come back every summer, for sure! Oh, it will break my heart to leave you,

Stony- I know; but my heart seems just
Lonesome bursting to go, too. An' you both
know I'd come back when you got
old an' needed me; an' then I'd
stay with you always!"

"Lyddy, Lyddy," exclaimed her
grandmother in a quivering voice,
"don't we need you now, an' all the
time? Think what it would be for
us if you took away the only sunshine that's left for us in Stony-Lonesome? As fur the mortgage,
it ain't nothing!"

But John Cassidy turned to the
man. "What do you know," he
asked harshly, "of the awful dangers,
an' the scarlet iniquities, an' all the
wrongs an' woes that crushes the
soul in a city? How fur have ye
ever been from Brine Settlement?"

"No furder 'n Halifax, Mr. Cassidy," said Job cheerfully, "'cept
maybe round the world onc't or
twic't when I was a lad an' followed
the sea!"

He paused in pardonable triumph; but as John Cassidy had no answer on his tongue, he went on: "An' I've found human natur' pretty much the same everywheres. I reckon 't ain't no worse in Bawston than in Brine Settlement, all in all!"

"You know," began Lydia excitedly, "now, while you an' gran'dad have each other, an' so well an' strong, and — and — young, in fact, now's the time for me to go —"

But at this point the look in her grandfather's face stopped her right short, her sentence dangling weakly in the air. Could he be a little — just a little — "touched" on the subject of Boston? she wondered. At least, she would drop the subject for the present, and await a more auspicious hour for resuming it. As she came to this conclusion, her grandmother spoke again.

"You're so young yet, Lyddy. Surely you can stay a bit longer in

Stony-Lonesome the old nest. Hain't the old folks got some claim on you yet?" she pleaded.

And Lydia, still glancing furtively and uneasily at her grandfather's face, replied: "Yes, dear. We won't talk any more about it now, — not this summer at all," she added, with sudden resolution, followed by a sigh.

John Cassidy could not trust himself to speak on the subject, so he proceeded to give Job directions about the afternoon's work. Dinner was done, and Lydia set herself to clearing the table.

John Cassidy wandered aimlessly about the kitchen, cutting his tobacco and filling his black clay pipe, till Lydia, having mixed a dish of potatoes and corn meal, went out to feed a coop of chickens back of the barn. Then he stood still in front of his wife.

"Oh, John, how are we goin' to

keep her to home without makin' *Stony-*
her feel as how she's in a prison?" *Lonesome*
moaned Mrs. Cassidy, rocking herself to and fro.

"That's the trouble, Marthy," said he slowly. "I can't bear to make her feel that way. An' she sees other girls goin'! An' oh, the rovin' spirit's in her blood! We must git her more books, an' let her go round more an' have a good time. I hain't quite understood her in the past, maybe."

"But she'll want to go next winter, John. An' we'll have to let her go, or she'll git to hate Stony-Lonesome an' fret herself to death."

"I'll see her dead," said John Cassidy slowly through white lips, "afore I'll let her go!" Then the fire smouldered down in his heart, and he went on: "But we'll try to wean her from it, Marthy; an' maybe God'll help us. He didn't help us much the other time, about Maggie,

Stony-Lonesome but maybe he'll hear us now. There's that organ the agent over to the Corners was tryin' to sell me. We'll git it. Lydia's been wantin' one this long time."

He stopped abruptly as Lydia came in with the empty dish. Putting a light to his pipe, he went out at once. Lydia had caught his last words, and now she saw her grandmother's eyes red and swollen. Her heart was torn with divided emotions. She was angry at the idea of being bribed, like a child, to give up what she looked upon as her serious ambitions. She told herself that the young had a right, a sacred right, to carve out their fortunes; and she was full of the idea that she had talents, — of just what nature she was hardly yet quite sure. At the same time, she loved her grandparents more deeply even than she herself suspected; and now, realizing as she had never done before the pain which she would cause them by her going, *Stony-Lonesome* she shrank at the thought of it. She did think of it, however, nearly all that night; and rising in the morning, dull-eyed, from a sleepless pillow, she told her grandparents that for a whole year, at least, she would say no more of Boston. Their joy was an illumination to her. A gladder sunshine seemed to stream down upon Stony-Lonesome, and she heard her grandfather whistling like a boy over his work in the corn-field. For days she herself had a calm, contented spirit, and turned her eyes no more to the notch in the hills.

It could not be expected that this contentment, reached so abruptly, should prove lasting. In a few weeks the young girl felt again the sting of the old restlessness. But she would not let it appear. In the autumn, when several girls of her acquaintance went away, full of sanguine enthusiasm, the gnawing fever in her veins

Stony-Lonesome grew almost intolerable. She fought it with a resolution which might have reassured John Cassidy as to her moral fibre; but it took its revenge by stealing from her cheeks the color and round young curves. The old people noted this, and grieved over it, and redoubled their furtive efforts to amuse her. Lydia wept at night over the struggle, but succeeded, after a time, in cultivating a cheery lightness of manner that deceived and relieved her grandparents. All through the spring and summer they grew more and more happily reassured; and all the time, under the restraint which she had put upon herself, the fire in Lydia's heart gathered heat.

At last, with the next coming of the fall, and the going of the birds, and the aching unrest which troubles the blood when the days grow short and chill with the diminishing year, Lydia could bear it no longer. She cried out to them one day, with a sudden storm of tears, that she must go away; that they must let her go for a little while, to come back to Stony-Lonesome in the spring. The poor little house of cards which the old people had been building all summer came straightway to the ground in piteous ruin.

Stony-Lonesome

John Cassidy said nothing. The look upon his face cut Lydia to the heart, but she hardened herself to meet it. It had been his rule, in bringing the girl up, to cross her wishes but rarely, and then with a finality that left no more to say. Now he shrank from entering into a direct conflict with her will. That his positive command would keep her at home, at least for the present, he knew; but he feared the ultimate result. With haggard eyes he gazed at Lydia for a few moments; then got up and went out. His wife set herself despairingly, with tears, and

Stony-Lonesome tender entreaties, and arguments which Lydia had already threshed over and over in her own mind, to turn the girl from her purpose. But Lydia was now in the full torrent of reaction from her long self-control, and neither argument nor entreaty could touch her. She fled to her own room, her handkerchief reduced to a wet and crumpled ball, her eyes red and angry. Throwing herself on her face upon the bed, she tried hard to fix her mind on such details as what clothes she would take with her and what time she would get away. She thought and thought, but her grandfather's haggard eyes kept thrusting themselves between her and her plans, till she sprang up and set herself feverishly to an examination of her wardrobe.

Down-stairs Mrs. Cassidy sat rocking to and fro, dropping hot tears upon the gray woolen sock which she was knitting. In her heart was a dark, half-realized phantom of a fear that her husband, in his anger, might do something dreadful to Lydia. She remembered that sudden, awful threat which had been wrung from him; and though she had lived with him these forty years, she did not even yet know the tenderness of his rugged heart. She trembled, and waited for what might happen.

Stony-Lonesome

John Cassidy came in, an hour later, and got his coat. He had harnessed up his old driving horse, and was going in to the Corners, — "to do an arr'nd," he said, in answer to his wife's query. In fact, he felt that he would have to get away from Stony-Lonesome in order to think clearly. He was bewildered by the problem which confronted him. But it was an unheard-of thing for him to go in to the Corners without taking Lydia along. The girl watched him from the window as the wagon

Stony-Lonesome went jolting down the lane, and read his bitterest rebuke in this solitary departure. It made her feel as if she were suddenly thrust out of his life. A keen foretaste of homesickness came over her.

As John Cassidy, with bent head and hands that scarcely felt the reins they held, moved along the quiet country road, his thoughts fell over one another in harassing confusion. At last, however, a definite purpose began to take shape. What if he should — quietly kill himself? If he were to throw himself from the wagon over some steep bank, on the way home that night, the world, or at least Brine Settlement, would call it an accident. And then Lydia would never have the heart to leave her widowed grandmother alone. John Cassidy shook at the thought, for he was a religious man, of the straitest sect of the Baptists. But after all, what, to him, was his own soul compared with Lydia's? He would take hell itself gladly, if thereby he might pluck Lydia from the brink. By the time he approached the Corners he had about made up his mind. He was planning the details minutely; and while this awful purpose, this incomparable heroism, was revolving in his brain, passers-by saw only a gray and weary-looking man bent over the reins, his eyes so fixed upon his horse's head that he hardly returned their salutations.

Still scrutinizing the dread burden in his heart, he went as usual to the post-office, and then to the village grocery for a bag of "feed." He tested the feed as critically, and questioned the price as frugally (gaining a few cents of discount because of a musty spot in the bag), as if he were just going home to fodder the cattle and make a hearty meal of buckwheat cakes. As he passed out of

Stony-Lonesome the shop, between a pile of codfish on one side and a dark-streaked molasses hogshead on the other, one of the group of men who occupied the counters and biscuit-boxes remarked to him, "I hear Lyddy's talkin' of goin' to Bawston this winter!"

John Cassidy glared blankly at the speaker, and went on without replying. When he was out of earshot a buzz of talk arose, and the old unhappy story of Lydia's mother was repeated, with many rustic embellishments.

But of the question and the questioner John Cassidy thought not at all. Just as he was getting into the wagon a new idea flashed upon his mind, and at once his whole plan fell to pieces. It occurred to him that if he were gone Lydia would soon coax her grandmother away to Boston. The cold sweat came out upon his forehead, as he saw how near he had been to throwing away his own soul, *Stony-* while, in the very act, thrusting *Lonesome* Lydia onward to a swifter ruin.

As he drove slowly along out of the village and into the wide, twilight country, his head drooped lower over the reins. It was characteristic of the measureless unselfishness of the man that now, though having, as he truly believed, just escaped with his soul, he was not glad. His brain lay dumb as a log in the blackness of dejection.

The country road was winding and variable, with here a swampy hollow and there a rocky steep. At last the moon came up, red, full, and distorted, and stared John Cassidy in the face. The jogging horse, the lean, high wagon, and the bent form on the seat cast grotesquely dancing shadows behind them. The naked stumps and rampikes cast other shadows, which pointed straight at John Cassidy in solemn stillness and with

Stony-Lonesome strange, unanimous meaning. The wagon reached a spot where the road was narrow, with a little bridge and a steep bank on one side. John Cassidy's face lit up. He stopped the horse, and looked down at the confusion of stones some six or eight feet below, with a rivulet prattling thinly just beyond them.

"If I kind of drop myself over there," said he, meditatively, "I ain't goin' to run no great resk o' killin' myself. No, sir! It'll break an arm or a leg, maybe, or put a shoulder out o' j'int, — enough to lay me up, that's all. With her grandfather a cripple," — here he winced, and looked around as if some one else had spoken the hated word in his ear, — "with me a cripple, I say," he repeated, obstinately, " Lydia could n't never think of goin' away."

He got out of the wagon, told the horse to go home, and struck him lightly with the whip. The animal looked around in wonder, and then obediently set forward, leaving his master standing by the roadside in the uncertain light.

"Even if I kin hold her back a year or so," mused John Cassidy, still looking down at the stones, "it's worth the while. She'll have sense, will Lydia, when she gits a little older. I wonder, now, if Job'll git the potatoes in all right 'thout my help, an' not mix the upland crop with them from the wet medder field?"

Now that he saw his way clear to the rescue of Lydia, the farmer's natural anxieties about the harvest again seized upon John Cassidy's mind; but only for an instant; the next he let himself topple over the bank, half-turning back as he fell, and clutching nervously at a wayside bush. The bush gave way at once, and he dropped heavily among the

Stony-Lonesome stones. In an instant he was on his feet again, staring around in a dazed way, and wondering how it was that he could stand up. Jumping to the conclusion that the fall had done him no injury, he made a start as if to climb back and try it again. But his knees failed, and he ground his teeth with a sudden pervading anguish, while the red moon seemed to reel and totter amid the tree-tops. Then consciousness faded from his brain.

Meanwhile the old horse had jogged faithfully homeward. The reins, slipping from the dashboard, trailed along the ground, till the horse turned in at the lane of Stony-Lonesome. Just then they caught and held on a projecting root, and the horse at once stopped. Half an hour later Job came down the lane to fetch water from the spring, and found the horse standing there patiently with the empty wagon behind him.

Job saw at once that something serious had happened. He ran perhaps a hundred yards along the road; then, realizing that he would be likely to need help, he sped back to the house for Lydia. Fearing to alarm Mrs. Cassidy, he asked the girl to take a step down the lane with him, it being such an "uncommon fine night." She was on the point of an abrupt refusal, when she caught the grave and anxious meaning in his eyes.

"All right, Job," said she, with a sudden vague apprehension. "I'll git my hat an' come right along."

She ran after the man, and overtook him halfway down the lane. "What's the matter?" she asked, breathlessly.

Job pointed to the horse and empty wagon, plainly visible a few rods below.

Stony-Lonesome "Where is he?" she gasped, clutching at Job's arm.

"Back along the road somewheres, likely," said Job. "I thought as how I might need help to lift him."

Lydia tried to question further, but the voice died in her aching throat, and she hurried on beside the man in stunned silence. A succession of dreadful forebodings flashed through her mind. She kept repeating to herself that she had killed her grandfather. Then they came to the wagon. Job turned the horse. She climbed to the wagon-seat, and sat with her fingers twisting and untwisting, as Job drove rapidly back along the road to the Corners.

The moon was higher and whiter now, and every object along the roadside stood out sharply. They came to the little bridge. They stopped, and cried out as with one voice when they saw John Cassidy's whip lying in the road. Then they sprang out of the wagon, and Lydia was down the bank in an instant, she knew not how. Kneeling in the edge of the stream, which she noticed not at all, she raised her grandfather's bleeding face to her bosom.

"Oh, he's alive! He breathes!" she cried in a high, breaking voice to Job, who was stooping over her.

When the old man had been carried home and laid in his own bed, he was still unconscious. Mrs. Cassidy, white and stern and tearless, took everything out of Lydia's hands, and astonished the girl by her swift energy and readiness. After what seemed weeks of waiting the doctor came. Having found a broken shoulder, he set it, and then announced that unless there was concussion of the brain the patient would almost certainly recover, though but slowly. Upon this Mrs. Cassidy went into another room, where she could not hear her husband's heavy breathing, and threw her apron over her face.

She had sat there for perhaps half an hour, when Lydia stole in to try and comfort her; but she turned on the girl bitterly. She was no longer the doting grandmother, but the grief-stricken wife, fierce at the pain which Lydia had caused her husband. By that deep intuition which may at times, we know not how, illumine a woman's heart, she saw that Lydia had been in some way the cause of the accident. And Lydia saw it, too, though there appeared to be no reasonable ground for such a conclusion. A few bitter words from the resentful woman, and Lydia also knew what had been so tenderly hidden from her,—the story of her mother's ruin. With bowed head and bleeding heart she crept back to her grandfather's bed, and crouched down beside it with her face buried in the quilt.

For days John Cassidy's life hung *Stony-* upon a thread. He was delirious *Lonesome* most of the time, and seeing Lydia's bright head so continually hanging over his pillow, his wanderings for the most part concerned themselves with her. From scattered phrases of his delirium and half-formed mutterings and appeals which wrung her soul, Lydia learned how little of accident there had been in the stroke which had overthrown her grandfather.

This knowledge, uncovering to her as it did the deeps of his devotion, pierced her with a pang that was not all pain. The remorseful anguish of it was lightened by the thought of such love enfolding her. This thought was like balm to the shame which had burned her spirit ever since that cruel revelation of her grandmother's. Under the scorching experiences of those grievous days Lydia's nature ripened.

On an afternoon of Indian sum-

Stony-Lonesome mer, one of those days when winter, though close at hand, seems to have fallen asleep and forgotten his purpose, Lydia stood again by the bars with her two pails of spring water. She gazed across the wide country to the mysterious notch in the hills. The patch of sky, melting in an indescribable violet haze, looked nearer than ever before, but it drew her not as before. She looked at it with a sort of pensive tenderness, the indulgence which one gives to a dream outgrown. Then she went back to the house, and presently up to her grandfather's bedside.

As she leaned over him, John Cassidy opened sane eyes and looked at her. The sickness had left his brain. Lydia gave a little sob of joy, fell on her knees, and dropped her face to the pillow beside his.

"Grandfather," she said, "I don't want any more to go away. I am going to live here always."

The tone, as much as the words, contented him. With a smile he moved his lips against her face for a moment, and then fell softly into a healing sleep.

Stony-Lonesome

THE END.